Welcome to…

The Hollywood Hills Clinic

Where doctors to the stars work miracles by day—
and explore their hearts' desires by night…

When hotshot doc James Rothsberg started the clinic six years ago he dreamed of a world-class facility, catering to Hollywood's biggest celebrities, and his team are unrivalled in their fields. Now, as the glare of the media spotlight grows, the Hollywood Hills Clinic is teaming up with the pro-bono Bright Hope Clinic, and James is reunited with Dr Mila Brightman…the woman he jilted at the altar!

When it comes to juggling the care of Hollywood A-listers with care for the underprivileged kids of LA *anything* can happen…and sizzling passions run high in the shadow of the red carpet. With everything at stake for James, Mila and the Hollywood Hills Clinic medical team, their biggest challenges have only just begun!

Find out what happens in the dazzling

The Hollywood Hills Clinic miniseries:

Seduced by the Heart Surgeon
by Carol Marinelli

Falling for the Single Dad
by Emily Forbes

Tempted by Hollywood's Top Doc
by Louisa George

Perfect Rivals…
by Amy Ruttan

The Prince and the Midwife
by Robin Gianna

His Pregnant Sleeping Beauty
by Lynne Marshall

And look out for another two titles from
The Hollywood Hills Clinic next month!

Dear Reader,

I was so pleased to say yes when I was asked to participate in The Hollywood Hills Clinic continuity! Not to mention that I smiled when I saw that my hero was both a prince *and* a doctor—probably not a usual combination, so I knew it would be a fun story to write.

This is the second book I've written with a midwife heroine—the first was for the Midwives On-Call at Christmas series I participated in. The other book—*Her Christmas Baby Bump*—was set in the UK, and this is in the US. There are quite a few interesting differences in midwifery between the two countries, which I found enjoyable to research.

My heroine here, in *The Prince and the Midwife*, works hard and keeps mostly to herself. Her emotions are still raw from a tragedy she hasn't put behind her. I loved the thought of my hero helping Gabby move from her painful past to a new future—but the journey isn't without a few bumps along the way.

Rafael has his own problems, and he's hiding out in LA for a while to deal with one of them—the constant media attention on a few scandals of his that the royal family is none too happy about. He's planning to steer clear of all women until the frenzy passes—but meeting Gabriella makes that feel impossible.

I enjoyed the sparks that fly between Gabby and Rafael from the moment they meet—though the initial sparks are mostly of the annoyed variety! But as they learn to respect one another's work they also learn that perhaps the way they've been living their lives isn't really what they want after all.

I hope you enjoy The Hollywood Hills Clinic books—and Rafael and Gabby's story. You can find out about my other stories, or contact me, at robingianna.com.

Happy reading!

Robin xoxo

THE PRINCE AND THE MIDWIFE

BY

ROBIN GIANNA

Published in Great Britain 2016
By Mills & Boon, an imprint of Harper Collins*Publishers*
1 London Bridge Street, London, SE1 9GF

Special thanks and acknowledgement are given to Robin Gianna for her contribution to The Hollywood Hills Clinic *series*

ISBN: 978-0-263-06471-1

Our policy is to use papers that are natural, renewable and recyclable products and made from wood grown in sustainable forests. The logging and manufacturing processes conform to the legal environmental regulations of the country of origin.

Printed and bound in Great Britain
by CPI Antony Rowe, Chippenham, Wiltshire

After completing a degree in journalism, then working in advertising and mothering her kids, **Robin Gianna** had what she calls her 'awakening'. She decided she wanted to write the kind of romance novels she'd loved since her teens, and now enjoys pushing her characters towards their own happily-ever-afters. When she's not writing, Robin fills her life with a happily messy kitchen, a needy garden, a wonderful husband, three great kids, a drooling bulldog and one grouchy Siamese cat.

Books by Robin Gianna

Mills & Boon Medical Romance

Midwives On-Call at Christmas

Her Christmas Baby Bump

Changed by His Son's Smile
The Last Temptation of Dr Dalton
Flirting with Dr Off-Limits
It Happened in Paris...
Her Greek Doctor's Proposal

Visit the Author Profile page at millsandboon.co.uk for more titles.

This book is dedicated to my friend and neighbour Betsy Hackett, RN, DSN. Thanks so much, Betsy, for putting up with my phone calls and numerous questions about midwifery and birthing babies—smooch!

Praise for
Robin Gianna

'Yet another splendid read from the author…a romance which should not be missed by everyone who loves medical romance.'

—*Harlequin Junkie* on
It Happened in Paris…

'The story flowed brilliantly, the dialogue was believable and I was thoroughly engaged in the medical dramas.'

—*Contemporary Romance Reviews* on
Changed by His Son's Smile

CHAPTER ONE

GABRIELLA CAIN ABSENTLY raked her fingers through her hair and stared at the messy room, fighting the deep fatigue that crept quietly into every aching muscle. Her second double shift of the week might be officially over, but as the labor suite department head she wasn't about to leave the disarray for the next midwife to clean up.

Thinking about the twins she'd just delivered to a Hollywood actress and the new mother's proud, beaming husband gave her an energy boost. The suite was a mess for a great reason—the birth of two healthy newborns. After all, just like a kitchen that was never cooked in stayed clean, a spic-and-span labor and delivery suite would mean no new little babies, and wouldn't that be a sad thing?

Gabby finished putting new sheets on the bed, wishing her own at home were as nice as the luxurious Egyptian cotton sheets The Hollywood Hills Clinic provided for its demanding patients, then topped it off with a fresh down blanket. The room was strewn with the various supplies she'd just used, and she figured it made sense to clean that up last so she could note what inventory she might be running low on and get them ordered tomorrow.

She folded clean blankets and stacked them inside the toasty warming cupboard. Crouching down to finally gather the things on the floor, the sound of the double swinging doors banging open and a gurney being hurriedly wheeled into the room had her pausing in surprise. The other, even more alarming sounds? A woman's moans and the receptionist shouting her name.

"Gabby? Gabby! Are you in here?" Stephanie called.

"I'm here." She stood and stared in dismay when she saw it was Cameron Fontaine lying on the gurney being steered by the hospital's uniformed EMTs, who had doubtless brought her here by helicopter. The famous A-list actress, who was one of Gabby's most difficult patients, and whose baby wasn't due for months. "Cameron? What's wrong?"

"I don't know. I think the baby's coming. It's way too soon, though, isn't it? Oh, God, I'm so scared." She jabbed her index finger toward Gabby, her blue eyes somehow wide with fear and imperiously demanding at the same time. "You've got to do something!"

Gabby's stomach plunged. Yes. It was too soon, and she sent up a deep prayer that Cameron wasn't in labor. That her baby would be fine. That her infant would be born healthy and alive. Her hands suddenly cold, she rushed over to wrap her fingers around Cameron's. "All right. Try to relax. Let's get you into the bed and see what's going on, okay?"

"Just get it stopped! The baby has to cook in there a little longer, right?"

Somehow, Gabby forced a smile, wishing it were that easy. "I believe the proverbial bun in the oven actually bakes, not cooks," she said lightly, proud that she'd managed to keep her tone joking and relaxed. "Let's see what we can do to make sure she gets to rise a little longer, hmm? Try not to worry until we learn more. Maybe baby is just in a mood, wanting a little attention?" She hoped that was the case, and resisted adding that would mean the infant was a chip off the old block.

Cameron's hand squeezed hers tightly, and Gabby frowned when she realized the woman's breath seemed short and gasping as the EMTs carefully moved her to the bed. Thirty-two weeks along was definitely not the optimal time for a baby to decide to come into the world.

"Stephanie, get in touch with whichever OB's on call and get them here, please."

Stephanie gave a nod and ran out, and Gabby barely noticed the EMTs leaving too as she grabbed the blood-pressure cuff. "I'm going to get your vital signs, then do an internal exam, okay?"

"Will you be able to tell if the baby's coming?"

"If you're dilating, yes. Tell me why you think you might be in labor. Are you in pain?"

"Not…not exactly pain." Cameron's hands cupped her belly and her face scrunched up in an unflattering expression Gabby was sure hadn't been seen on any movie screens by the actress's many fans, which proved how distressed she was. "I felt a little crampy, kind of like the Braxton-Hicks contractions you talked to me about. And my belly got sort of hard, and when it didn't go away I knew I had to do something right away and called the clinic."

"You did exactly the right thing, calling for the helicopter to come get you."

"Well, it seemed to take them forever!" She swiped her elegantly manicured hand across her frowning brow. "It was at least five minutes longer than when they came to get me after I hit my head, and every second that passed I got more worried. I called three times, and I think that made them finally hurry."

A smile touched Gabby's lips, as it was pretty easy to

imagine how those conversations had gone. "Let's see how baby is doing, all right?"

Gabby pressed her stethoscope to Cameron's belly, and the sound of the baby's steady heartbeat sent the breath she was holding right out of her lungs. Thank God, baby was still alive and moving. She snapped on exam gloves and what she found during the examination was a mixed blessing. "The good news is that your membranes are still intact, so no rupture there. Which means your labor's not advanced, which is also good news. But your cervix is dilated two centimeters, so we're going to have to do something about that."

"Like what? And what do you mean, labor's not advancing? Dilating means labor, right?"

Cameron's voice had gone a little shrill, and who could blame her? Gabby knew she had to help her stay calm—the situation was scary, yes, but with luck it could be managed. "Dilation means early labor, yes, but it can be slowed or sometimes completely stopped with medication. I'm going to get an IV set up to give you a mag sulfate drip right away, and also keep you hydrated with saline and lots of water to drink. We'll do a urinalysis to make sure there's no infection, just to be safe. Then we'll give you steroid injections to help baby's lungs develop in case she decides she just can't wait to get here. Please, try not to worry, okay? We'll be doing all we can to keep her healthy."

"I want to see Dr. Crane. When is she coming?"

Gabby had learned long ago to not be insulted by that demand, which she got from a lot of patients and their husbands. And when it came right down to it, she wanted the obstetrician to get there, too, in case the situation got worse instead of better. "I'll find out." She patted Cameron's shoulder and smiled. "Try to relax. Easy to say, I know, but you don't want your blood pressure all out of whack and make things tougher for baby, do you?"

"Could you get me something to drink before you leave? My breath's been so short for what seems like hours, and I'm beyond parched." She wrapped her fingers around her throat, little gasping sounds coming from her mouth that this time sounded a little forced. "I'd love some artesian sparkling water with a squeeze of lime. You have that, of course, don't you?"

Gabby wanted to say it was more important to get going on the medications she needed first, before wetting her whistle, but figured it would be just as fast to get what Cameron wanted as to point that out.

The small stainless-steel refrigerator in every room was kept well stocked, and Gabby ran the lime wedge around the rim of the crystal glass like a Hollywood Hills nurse who'd been a former bartender had taught her to. Cameron grabbed it like she'd been walking miles through the desert, and Gabby was glad after all that she'd taken a moment to get it for her.

"I'll be right back, okay?" Gabby hurried out to find Stephanie, passing through the halls and out past the beautiful fountain in the center of the glass atrium that made the place feel like a luxury hotel, and breathed in the calming scents of lavender and sandalwood. Except at that moment it didn't do much to slow the current surge of adrenaline that had replaced all her prior fatigue.

"Is the doc on the way to see Cameron, Stephanie? Who is it?"

"Well, as I was about to see who's on call, James phoned. He told me Cameron contacted him while she was on the helicopter to tell him to send her own doctor, because she's convinced Dr. Crane is our best. But she's out of town, so James asked a good friend of his who's in L.A. visiting to come see her. A Dr. Rafael Moreno."

"What?" Gabby stared at her, not comprehending. "Some friend of his? What do you mean?"

"I guess he's some world-renowned OB, and not only that but the prince of some Mediterranean principality, if you can imagine. Isn't that exciting?" Stephanie's eyes were shining, which seemed ridiculous to Gabby since the woman saw superstars in this hospital all the time. "Said he has privileges in hospitals all over the world, including here in California, and thinks Cameron would appreciate the status of having a prince taking care of her."

Gabby gaped. *What in the world?* A *prince* OB? Just visiting the U.S.? *That* was who James thought was the best person to care for this very demanding and famous patient?

She loved working at The Hollywood Hills Clinic but just might have to point out to James Rothsberg that, exclusive and prestigious or not, the number one focus at this hospital still had to be on premier medical care and not the royalty status of some doctor from another country he happened to be besties with. And, yes, she knew James had founded this hospital with that philosophy, demanding every patient receive the best medical care available, but had to wonder about this particular decision.

"Well, send him in as soon as he gets here, please." She headed back to the room, pondering if she should call James right then to talk to him about the seriousness of Cameron's situation and ask about this doctor and his qualifications—if he was really "world renowned," or just famous for being royal.

"The doctor's on the way, Cameron," she said as she got the items she needed. "I'm going to start your IV now." For the moment, she had to ignore the last of the mess in the room she hadn't finished cleaning up yet until the doctor arrived and she was certain Cameron had been stabilized.

"It'd better be Dr. Crane," Cameron said, looking away at the wall with a dramatic wince and yelp as Gabby got the IV needle placed in her arm. "She already knows all about me and my past health scares and situation and I only want to see her."

"I know you do." Gabby tried to find reassurance in the fact that Cameron's voice had become the petulant one she often used when she felt normal. At least she wasn't getting real contractions yet or freaking out. Gabby conjured her own acting skills and infused her voice with enthusiasm, bracing herself for the woman to get upset at the news her doctor was unavailable. "Unfortunately Dr. Crane is out of town. But this doctor is a personal friend of James Rothsberg and is not only an excellent OB but apparently a prince too."

"A prince?" Surprise lit Cameron's face before it relaxed into a pleased smile, thank heavens, instead of outrage. "Well, how nice. If Dr. Crane can't be here, at least a prince will understand how important my baby is to the world."

Because a prince and a self-absorbed actress's baby were more important to the world than most other human beings? Emotions crowded Gabby's chest—disbelief that Cameron obviously genuinely believed that. Annoyance with that attitude. And deeply buried pain. Because every person's baby was the most important child on earth to them.

She swallowed before she spoke. "I'm not sure when Dr. Moreno is going to get here, and we shouldn't wait to get your mag sulfate drip started. Is your belly still hard and tight? Still feeling crampy?"

"Well, yes. But not too bad. I think we should wait for this prince-doctor." She picked up the television remote, clicked to a movie channel, and beamed the famous megawatt smile she normally reserved for the cameras. "Oh, look, it's one of mine! I loved this one!"

"Cameron." Gabby worked to keep her patience. "Giving you the sulfate drip certainly isn't going to hurt, regardless of what Dr. Moreno has to say, and timing can be critical. Up to three courses of steroids are recommended for the baby's lung health, but have to be given at least twenty-four hours apart, and the sooner we give the first one, the sooner we can give the second one."

"I admit I'm still nervous. I know you're good at what you do. If you think you need to start it now, then let's do it." Cameron's smile disappeared, and Gabby's frustration with her patient evaporated when she saw the tension etched on her face. Probably her wanting to wait and watch the movie, all smiles, was some coping mechanism, telling herself everything was fine now that she was here at the clinic. Deluding oneself was all too easy to do, as Gabby knew firsthand.

She patted Cameron's arm, then gave it a gentle squeeze. "I'll get it started right now. And I bet the doctor will be here any moment." As though her words had willed it, a brisk knock on the door sounded, and she turned as it opened.

To reveal the most physically beautiful man she'd ever seen.

His dark hair was cut fairly short and impeccably groomed, and his olive skin was tanned a golden brown which looked even more swarthy in contrast to his white doctor's coat. The blue dress shirt he wore was crisply starched but left open at the collar without a tie, and it was obvious that beneath it lay a very well-built physique. But the most riveting thing about him was the startling color of his eyes, nearly the same hue as springtime in Seattle after rains had turned the landscape a vivid green.

She felt a little as though all the oxygen had been sucked from the room as those eyes met hers. Though the contact was brief, his gaze seemed to both assess her and dismiss her at the same time. Then his attention moved around the room in a careful scan of the space before finally focusing on their patient.

A smile transformed the aloof expression on his handsome face. *"Buenos días."* He stepped to the bed, reached for their patient's hand and, to Gabby's astonishment, lifted it to his lips. Since when did doctors kiss their patients, even if it was just on the hand? "I do not have to ask if you are the famous Cameron Fontaine. I would recognize your stunning face anywhere. I am Dr. Rafael Moreno."

"It's wonderful to meet you, Doctor," Cameron practically cooed.

"I understand your very special baby is demanding some unexpectedly early attention. I'm told your little one is a girl—what a lucky child. She'll no doubt be as beautiful as you are." Lord. Gabby had to wonder if he'd intentionally ratcheted up the charm, or if it just oozed naturally from the man. "Let us see what she has in mind, shall we?"

"Yes. I'm so anxious to hear what you think is going on and what to do about it."

Cameron's expression could only be described as coy and flirtatious, and Gabby caught herself about to shake her head at the whole scene. Dr. Moreno had instantly sized the woman up, that was for sure, and Gabby was torn between admiration and disgust at how quickly and easily he'd had her eating out of his hand. While not even bothering to introduce himself to Gabby or ask who she was. The man was royal, all right. Royally rude.

"Tell me what's been happening." He sat and directed

his attention solely to Cameron, as though Gabby wasn't even there, and the actress told him all about her symptoms as he looked at the vital signs Gabby had recorded. He took his time speaking with her, acting more like they were at a cocktail party than in a hospital room. But of course Cameron, who was always more than happy to talk at length about herself, basked in the attention as he asked all kinds of questions about her life and career in addition to the ones related to her health.

As the minutes stretched on, Gabby fidgeted, wondering when in the world he was going to get on with what needed to be done and have her administer the meds Cameron needed. At the same time, she had to grudgingly give him credit for completely relaxing their patient.

Then that credit evaporated when he reached for gloves, obviously planning to give her an internal exam.

"Excuse me, Dr. Moreno, but did you see in the chart that I just gave her an exam about thirty minutes ago? That she was already dilated to two centimeters?" Gabby asked.

He turned to her with one eyebrow quirked. "And you are…?"

"I'm Gabriella Cain, head midwife here at The Hollywood Hills Clinic."

"Now that I am here to care for Ms. Fontaine, I will take care of future internal exams. I'm sure you know they need to be limited in cases of early onset labor."

What the…? Anger began to burn in Gabby's chest. "Yes, I am aware of that, Dr. Moreno. Which is why I feel you should wait to do another. I was about to get the mag sulfate drip started, followed by the steroids, then do an ultrasound."

"I prefer to not rely on others' examinations and opinions, as that normally isn't in the best interests of my patient. However, if you've done an internal exam, I won't do another at the moment." He turned away from Gabby again, and she stared at the back of his silky dark head, hardly able to believe his arrogantly dismissive attitude. *His* patient? She'd worked with some doctors with domineering attitudes before, but this guy got first place for jerk of the year.

"It's good that you're dilated to no more than two centimeters," he said to Cameron as he looked at Gabby's notes. "Although that is clearly an indication of pre-term labor, there are things we can do to try to make that cease, and at the same time give baby a chance to grow more."

"So it is preterm labor. I was so hoping it wasn't." Cameron's white teeth worried her lip, her eyes wide. "Do you think whatever you do to try to stop it will work?"

"It often does, so we will hope for the best." He lifted his tall frame from the stool he'd been perched on, moving to stand beside the bed and hold Cameron's hand between both of his, a smile on his face some people might think was charming. "And if baby says, *Oh, no, Mama, I'm coming anyway*, we will at least have time to give you steroids to help her little lungs function better when she arrives. So we will do that without delay. Okay?"

"All right. Whatever you think," Cameron said, all grateful smiles. "Thank you so, so much, Doctor."

"Please, call me Rafael."

Whatever you think. Thank you so, so much... Gabby gritted her teeth and told herself she couldn't feel bothered by Cameron's immediate agreement to the same treatment she'd initially refused to agree to when Gabby had told her exactly the same thing. It was no secret doctors got more respect than midwives from many patients, and an über-handsome doctor who, by the way, happened to be a prince too? Jerk or not, it was no surprise that status-conscious Cameron was all too happy to go along with whatever he suggested.

"Bien." He stood and turned to Gabby, and his warm expression cooled to one of professionalism. "I'd assume you have the mag sulfate and steroid ready?" Those startling green eyes slowly scanned the area again before pinning hers again with one dark eyebrow raised. "Except perhaps I should not assume that. When I first walked in I was shocked to see the state of this room, which is, well, I must say, terribly disorganized. I'm frankly very surprised by this, considering the stellar reputation of The Hollywood Hills Clinic and knowing James Rothsberg's perfectionism."

The irritation that had been simmering in her chest burst into a full conflagration of anger that surged through her blood and made her brain burn. Who did this guy think he was? Friend or no friend of James, prince or no prince, he had no right to waltz in like he owned the place, give it his version of the white-glove test, then criticize her without knowing a thing about the patients and medical situations she'd been taking care of for the past ten hours.

"I was in the process of cleaning and reorganizing it from an earlier, lengthy delivery when Cameron arrived in what might have been an emergency situation. I deemed taking care of her and her baby was a lot more important than tidying and prepping a room that could be tidied and prepped later. And the meds *are* ready."

She stalked to the counter, gathering the items together and wishing she could throw them at his arrogant, judgmental face. He reached for them, his hand briefly touching hers, and it ticked her off even more that the feel of his skin brushing hers sent some kind of weird electric shimmer up her arm. The sensation could have been mistaken for attraction, if there had been anything attractive about the man.

Well, there were all those superficially attractive things, but she wasn't a woman interested in slick, glossy men. Or any kind of man anymore, really.

With grudging respect, though, Gabby did have to admire how quickly and efficiently his long fingers administered the drugs, all the while keeping up a smoothly distracting conversation with their patient.

"All set," he said to Cameron, giving her a warm and reassuring smile. "Now we wait, keep you comfortable, and check baby periodically through ultrasound and monitoring."

"Thank you, Rafael. I'm *so* glad you and Gabby are the ones taking care of me."

And Gabby was glad the next shift midwife would be arriving soon to deal with Cameron and Dr. Moreno. Not to mention that she was way overdue for a major nap.

"How about deciding what you'd like to have for dinner?" Gabby said as she brought her another sparkling water, along with a menu of options for her meal. The onsite Michelin-starred chef was amazing, and even the pickiest patients loved the elegant and trendy foods he prepared. "The midwife on the next shift will be checking on you throughout the night to make sure you're comfortable. Then tomorrow morning I'll be back to take care of you. In the afternoon it'll be time to administer another steroid dose."

"But I don't want another midwife," Cameron said, a twisting pout on her lips that had Gabby wondering how in the world she managed to still look so pretty doing it. "I want you to stay here with me tonight, Gabby."

The fatigue Gabby had felt earlier was back in spades. She had a feeling if she closed her eyes she might fall asleep on her feet like a horse, and the vision of curling up in her own comfy bed and getting a solid night's sleep nearly had her moaning, but she knew Cameron. And Cameron's expectations. The Hollywood Hills Clinic was known for its exceptional medical care, and that included going above and beyond in every way.

Which meant she'd be spending the night here again.

"I appreciate you wanting me with you, Cameron. I—"

"Your staying here is important, since you are familiar with our special patient and her physical condition and worries," Rafael interrupted smoothly. "Here is my contact information. Please don't hesitate to get in touch with me for any reason."

Did the man think he was boss of the world? Gabby felt like smacking that seemingly sincere smile from his handsome face as he handed her an elegantly embossed card, then turned to give one to their patient. When Cameron reached for hers, she clasped his hand along with it for a lingering moment, practically batting her long lashes at him as she smiled back.

"Thank you so much, Rafael. I can't tell you how much I appreciate your help and expertise during this terrifying time."

"It's beyond my pleasure. It is my calling to help mamas and their babies, whether a pregnancy is smooth and uneventful or high risk and worrying. I promise to take care of you and *bebé* to the best of my ability."

Whereas Gabby and most other nurses and doctors didn't? The guy was pure egotistical arrogance in a white coat, absolutely no doubt about that. And Gabby intended to tell him so, though somehow she'd have to tone down the strength of the language she'd really like to use when she did.

"As I started to say a moment ago, Cameron, I'm more

than happy to stay," she said, giving Dr. Moreno a pointed look she hoped he interpreted correctly—which was to tell him to keep his guest-in-this-hospital nose in his own business. "I'll sleep better knowing I can check regularly on how you're doing, and hopefully me being here will help you sleep better too."

"Thank you, Gabby. I will sleep better."

"Why don't you rest now and watch a little TV? I'll be back in a few minutes to find out what you've decided to order for dinner." She turned to Dr. Full-of-Himself and somehow kept her voice cordial. "May I speak to you privately in my office, Dr. Moreno?"

He inclined his head again, and she sensed him following her from the room and down the marble-tiled hallway, past large windows with beautiful views Gabby normally enjoyed, but not at that moment. Right then, she had only one thing on her mind, which was giving Rafael Moreno a piece of it.

She stopped in front of the open door of her office and gestured for him to go inside but he stopped with her.

"Ladies first," he said as he mirrored her gesture.

A man with good manners was usually appealing, but this didn't feel like good manners. It felt more like he was just being controlling again, wanting things to be the way he wanted them and not giving her respect for the fact that it was *her* office. Which meant she should be calling the shots at that moment, even if it was something as simple as who entered the room first.

The smile she stuck on her face was stiff and fake and she didn't care if he saw through it. While part of her knew it wasn't something worth arguing about, he'd irritated her so much already she found herself digging in her heels. "No, I insist. You are a guest here at the clinic, after all." And if that didn't give him a strong hint that he'd overstepped his bounds, she was about to tell him so much more directly.

Those silky eyebrows rose at her, and their gazes clashed for several heartbeats until he inclined his head and stepped into the room. She shut the door behind her, not wanting anyone to overhear their conversation, and when she turned to look at him she had that oxygen-sucked-from-the-room feeling again. His height and the breadth of his shoulders made the room seem to shrink, and his erect posture and the utter self-assurance of his demeanor compounded the effect until she felt she couldn't breathe.

Except breathing was necessary to give him a piece of her mind. Her mouth suddenly dry as sandpaper, she hoped he couldn't sense her discomfiture as she stepped behind her desk instead of having them sit in the two chairs side by side, wanting to send another message that she was in charge of the maternity wing and its midwives and he should treat her accordingly.

"Please sit," she said as she perched herself in her swivel chair.

But of course he didn't. He simply stared down at her, and she suddenly felt like a bug-eyed hamster being eyed by a hawk. Rafael Moreno, standing there all confident and imperious, had utterly ruined the message she'd tried to send by sitting behind the desk, so now what was she supposed to do? Sit there craning her neck up at him while giving him a dressing-down? Or bob back up like a jack-in-the-box? Either one would make her look foolish and, worse, completely lacking in power and authority.

Damn the man.

"What is it you wish to discuss with me, Ms. Cain?"

She huffed out a breath, trying hard to regain some semblance of equilibrium, and slowly stood again to look him in the eye. Or as much as that was possible, considering he still had a good six or seven inches in height on her. "I know you are James's friend, and I'm told you are good at what you do. Also that you are part of a royal family, which is perhaps why you feel you can do as you please."

"I can do as I please."

The arrogance of the words wasn't diminished by the even modulation of his deep voice. Her heartbeat upped its tempo to double time, and that burning sensation prickled her scalp again. "Maybe you can in a lot of places, but not here, Dr. Moreno. I may be a midwife and not a physician, but I assure you that I'm the person in charge of the day-to-day operation of The Hollywood Hills Clinic's maternity ward. While I am grateful you came quickly to see Cameron when James requested you to, I don't appreciate you walking in and just taking over. Completely ignoring the notes I made on Ms. Fontaine's chart and utterly dismissing my medical opinion and recommendation. Even worse, you said and did it all in front of the patient. That was insulting and rude, and frankly could have very well undermined her confidence in me, my knowledge, and my skills."

The expression on his smooth, angular features didn't change, but in the depths of his eyes there was a sudden, dangerous glint. Her breath caught and held in her chest during the long pause that crackled between them before he finally spoke. "Anything else?"

"Yes, actually."

Gabby slowly walked around from behind the desk, taking that moment to get the air moving in her lungs again, hoping to calm both her tripping heart and her frustration. For the first time in her life she wished she was taller than her five feet six inches, but was so angry she came to stand nearly toe to toe with him anyway.

"I resent you saying that room was a mess, that it was substandard, and by association that *I'm* substandard. Even worse that you said it in front of our patient as well. I work very hard to keep my ward immaculately clean, organized and running smoothly, to keep these rooms as luxurious and beautiful as James insists they be, and our patients expect. But as an obstetrician you should certainly know that when there's any kind of medical emergency, like the difficult twin births I was dealing with prior to Cameron arriving, it tends to mess up a hospital room. Is it possible that you never give that a thought, though, since an OB can often run in, catch a baby, play hero, then leave the cleanup to someone else?"

"I assure you," he said in a silky-soft voice at odds with that glint sparking in his eyes, "I am well versed in hospital room chaos, having worked in all kinds of clinics around the world. *I* resent *your* implication that I'm a spoiled and selfish man unwilling to take on any task required of me. That is an unacceptable insult. Who and what I am is a doctor who prides himself on paying attention to every detail, and the fact is that the disarray of that room was obvious evidence that I had to take control of the situation."

The small gap between them closed, and with his narrowed gaze so close, so intense Gabby found she had to break their eye contact before she got dizzy from it. Which then had her staring at his mouth, at lips that were hard and uncompromising, and somehow at the same time so soft and sensually shaped that her stomach did a strange little flip that didn't feel at all like the anger pumping through her veins.

"And I assure you that was a misconception, and you *taking control of the situation* was both unnecessary and unwelcome." Gabby resisted the urge to stroke her hand down her throat, swiping away the sweat she was sure must be forming there. Why did it suddenly seem so hot in this room? Was it her anger making her heart quiver, and was it her imagination that all that heat seemed to be shimmering right between them, practically pouring from his big, masculine body? "If you end up coming back to see Cameron, and I frankly would prefer a different physician do so, I would appreciate you showing me respect in front of our patient, and I will continue to show you that same respect."

"Oh, I'll be back, Ms. Cain, have no doubt about that. Whether you like it or not. When I make a commitment to a friend like James, and to a patient, I always see it through to the end." His eyes were still narrowed, his words still spoken in that silky, soft tone that sounded odd, coming from lips that had been firmly clamped together the whole time she'd spoken. Then, to her utter shock, he reached for her hand and lifted it to those beautiful lips, pressing them to the back of it.

Both soft and firm, he kept them there for three long seconds, causing that weirdly disconcerting spark to fly up her arm again. Then he released it and, without another word, turned and strode out the door.

Gabby stared blindly at the wall beside her door, absently running her palm from the back of her other hand up her arm, feeling the gooseflesh still making all the little hairs stand at attention. "Well, Gabby, that went well," she muttered to herself, barely able to catch her breath. "When it comes to verbal sparring to handle a problem, that man is clearly way out of your league."

Which left her with a very difficult question. What she was going to do next to keep him from taking over her entire ward?

CHAPTER TWO

"YOU'VE ALWAYS BEEN a workaholic, but your schedule seems insane to me," Rafael said as he sat across from James, glad his friend had finally found time to stop by the cliffside home Rafael was renting. "I thought I might be moving on from L.A. before we had a chance to share another drink."

"Hey, I do things other than work."

"Like what? Are you taking up golf?" Rafael asked with a grin, since he knew the man had zero interest in spending that much time on a game.

That drew a return grin from James. "No, but I do have a date in about…one hour," he said, glancing at his watch. "And what do you mean, you might be moving on from L.A. soon? Is rolling stone Rafael already thinking about leaving? I thought you'd come here to go into hiding for a while."

"Doesn't seem to have worked too well. One or the other of my parents calls me practically daily with disapproving updates on the photos and completely exaggerated stories still showing up in the gossip magazines about me."

"If you didn't date strippers, maybe you wouldn't have that problem."

"I didn't even know she'd been a stripper until it was splashed across all the papers." He shook his head, wondering why everyone had to make such a big deal out of it anyway. "But if I hear one more word from my family about having to find a 'suitable' girlfriend, I may just become a monk."

"Like there's any chance of that," James said with a smirk. "One of the reasons I always liked hanging out with you was because women flock around a prince like ants to a piece of candy. A good way for me to meet the cast-offs."

"Because you have such a problem with meeting women," Rafael said dryly. "Didn't you just tell me you have a date tonight?"

"Yeah." James's face instantly settled into an oddly serious expression, and it struck Rafael that his friend might be getting back into a relationship with Mila Brightman, his former fiancée.

"I heard you're having to spend time with Mila now you're working with her charity," he said casually, hoping James would talk to him about it if he felt a need to. "Are you seeing her again?"

"No. That was over long ago." James seemed to be studying the condensation droplets on his iced-tea glass very intently, and Rafael wondered if it was to avoid looking him in the eye. "But I do think dating someone new is a good idea to, you know, distract me from thinking about the past."

Rafael frowned. He knew their breakup had been hard on both James and Mila, but it had been James's idea, after all. How much was he still bothered by it? "Maybe you and Mila—"

"I don't really want to talk about it." James set his glass down and put on the cool, professional face Rafael had seen many times when James wanted to put distance between himself and others. "Tell me about how things went with Cameron Fontaine. And by the way, I don't think I've told you how much I appreciate you seeing her."

"I'm glad you asked me. It's what I do. Not to mention that not working and having to lie low in L.A. has been getting a little tedious, so I'm happy to be at the clinic." Oddly, the first thing James's question instantly brought to mind wasn't his patient but a certain gorgeous midwife who was an all-too-attractive combination of warmth and smarts and toughness.

Thinking back, he realized he'd deserved the one-two punch she'd given him in her office. He should have shown her immediate respect instead of making her earn it, but in some of the places he'd worked, it had been important to make sure everyone knew what they were doing before you trusted them to. In spite of the chaotic condition of the room, it had been obvious that she was an expert when it came to the medical care of the patients. And wasn't afraid to point it out in no uncertain terms to anyone who doubted that.

"What's with that smile on your face?" James asked, quirking his eyebrow. "Did you fall in lust with Cameron?"

"No." That would be a snowy day in the desert, and he practically laughed at the question. Cameron Fontaine was the kind of self-absorbed woman he met all too often and had no interest in even for just sex.

He wouldn't admit to James that the woman he'd felt a stirring of lust for had been the clinic's head midwife. A woman with a fiery temper to match the golden fire of her hair. The last thing he needed was the complication of dating someone he had to work with. Not to mention that dating anyone at that particular moment was asking for more trouble from the press and anger and disapproval from his family.

After the tabloids had blown up again with the juicy

story of his latest girlfriend, his parents had insisted he stop embarrassing them. It all seemed so ridiculous since he'd dated the woman barely a month before they'd stopped seeing each other, which was how he liked to keep it. Any longer than that and a woman had a tendency to start thinking long term, and he had no intention of doing forever after with anyone. His brother had taken care of marrying to provide heirs, and saddled himself with a woman who didn't even like him much. And the picture-perfect partnership of his parents' arranged marriage? It didn't hint at the cool distance between them, or question why they were on different continents half the time.

No, Rafael was never going to get stuck in some passionless marriage. He liked his freedom and planned to keep it, thank you very much. Lying low to let his parents simmer down a little was the price he had to occasionally pay for that freedom. With any luck, they'd soon stop throwing "suitable" women his way, wanting to torture him with the kind of loveless marriage they had.

"I'm not sure we're going to be able to stop Cameron's labor," he told James, "but I'm hoping to be able to get her at least a second steroid dose before it happens. I'm heading over there soon to see how she's doing."

"Good. You're the best at what you do, and I hope she knows that. I'm guessing she doesn't mind that her doctor is a prince either."

Probably true, but his royal status was something Rafael found to be a far bigger burden than a benefit. "I'll text you with an update after I see her."

"I'd appreciate that." James stood, so Rafael did too. "I'd better get cleaned up for my date."

He had to wonder how Mila would react to seeing photos of James with a doubtless beautiful woman in the media that followed him around as much as they followed him, but it wasn't any of his business.

No, his present business was to keep a low profile and his own face out of the tabloids for as long as possible.

Gabby poured herself another cup of coffee, desperate to somehow keep her heavy eyelids from closing. During the night, when Cameron had slept, she'd managed to grab an hour or two of rest, but had jumped to attention every time Cameron had woken up, both worried that her labor might be advancing. That, combined with her recent double shifts prior to Cameron's arrival, had left her without much in the way of reserve energy.

Gulping at the dark, hot liquid, Gabby moved to Cameron's bedside again. "Any changes in the way you're feeling?"

"No." Cameron folded her arms across her chest and pouted up at Gabby. "And I'm awfully tired of just lying here. The only thing that makes it bearable at all is the good care you're taking of me."

"That's nice of you to say." Her words managed to fractionally perk Gabby up since, inside, she'd become a little tired of catering to the woman's every whim. At least she apparently appreciated it. "I'm doing everything I can to keep you comfortable, and hopefully help baby stay in there a little longer."

"I know I should apologize for being a tad complaining. Even grumpy occasionally. It's just so tiresome being in this bed, but I know you understand that."

"I do understand. Would you like your pillows plumped again?"

At her nod, Gabby complied, thinking it was good the pillows were faux down to prevent any allergens from being in the room, as real down would have been plumped to death by now. Cameron's word "tad" was an understatement, but Gabby was pretty sure the woman truly didn't realize that "Diva" should be her middle name.

"It's not easy getting comfortable, sitting in a bed all day, or to keep from getting bored. I'll bring you another book to read, if you like."

"Maybe later." She leaned back against her pillows with a long-suffering sigh. Just as Gabby was about to creep away, Cameron opened her eyes and started talking again. "And of course the other thing making it bearable to be here is Rafael. He's just the sweetest, dreamiest thing, don't you think? And he's obviously a wonderful doctor."

Dreamy, maybe, when it came to his looks. But sweet? Definitely not. It was an effort, but Gabby managed to keep a smile on her face and sort of agree. "He has an excellent reputation. I'm glad you like him."

"Like him? I just love him! Adore him!" Cameron gushed. "I feel so lucky that he happens to be in Los Angeles right now. It seems like fate, doesn't it?"

Privately, she didn't think it was fate, unless the universe had decided to challenge Gabby by making life at the clinic difficult, having to work with someone as full of himself as Rafael Moreno. But she was a professional and could handle it, no matter what. And, to look at the positive, at least Cameron was happy.

She glanced at her watch. "If you're not going to sleep right now, I'd like to get another ultrasound of baby, then give your next steroid injection."

"Should we wait for Rafael?" Anxious blue eyes met hers. "He said he'd be here this afternoon, and I'm sure he will be."

Damn the man for insisting he be in charge of everything, and basically telling the patient not to trust her. "I believe Dr. Moreno was simply being cautious because he doesn't personally know me. But midwives are highly trained in all aspects of pregnancy and delivery, including caring for high-risk patients. You can trust me completely."

"Of course I trust you. In fact I'm— I— Oh, my God!" Cameron sat bolt upright in bed, her eyes suddenly wide and scared as she stared at Gabby.

Her heart picked up speed because the look on Cameron's face didn't seem like overdramatic acting this time. She reached for Cameron's hand. "What? What is it?"

"I think...I think my waters just broke!"

Oh, no. Gabby immediately checked to be sure Cameron wasn't experiencing some other sensation that made her think it was her membranes breaking, but there was no doubt about it.

Heart sinking, she prayed the steroids had gotten baby's lungs developed enough for the premature infant to be all right. She perched on the side of the bed and reached for Cameron's hands again. "You're right. Your waters have broken, which means your amniotic sac is no longer intact. And that means baby has to be born, otherwise there's risk of infection. I'll call Dr. Moreno and get him here right away."

"Oh, yes, you must!" Cameron's manicured nails dug into Gabby's skin. "Tell him it's an emergency!"

"I'm sure he'll get here as quickly as possible. Try not to worry, okay? With luck, you'll have a smooth, uncomplicated delivery, and baby will be just fine. I'll be right back."

Gabby managed to extricate her hands from Cameron's grip and made a quick note of the time her waters had broken and an estimation of the amount of fluid before she moved into the hallway to pull up Dr. Moreno's number on her cell. Hopefully, he wasn't at lunch with some bigwig, or with a woman after a date the night before and not answering the phone because of it. And why that thought would make her tummy tighten uncomfortably, she had no idea. Must just be concern for Cameron, because she knew the woman would worry about having a different doctor come to deliver the baby.

But he answered after only two rings, and Gabby let out a relieved breath. "Dr. Moreno, it's Gabby Cain. Cameron's waters broke a few minutes ago and—"

"I'll be right there."

She stared at the now dead phone. Now, there was a man of few words. And questions. Which was probably a good thing since the sooner he arrived, the sooner he'd wield his potent charm on Cameron to keep her calmer in a way Gabby wasn't always able to accomplish.

Back in Cameron's room, she plumped her pillows yet again and checked her vital signs once more. "Dr. Moreno's on his way."

"I knew he'd come right away. I'm just praying he gets here before my baby does!"

"It usually takes a while for contractions to get strong enough for baby to be born. Are you feeling any yet?"

"I…I can't tell for sure. I feel very crampy, like there's a fist inside my belly. It doesn't feel good. And my back really aches. Is it going to get worse? I hate pain! I don't do well with it at all!"

The famous blue eyes staring at her were so scared and anxious Gabby gave her hands another reassuring squeeze. "How contractions feel varies a lot from woman to woman. Some go from feeling cramps that become more intense as labor progresses, and others experience pretty intense contractions. But all that is helping your baby be born, so it's nothing to be afraid of."

"How long will it take?"

"That varies too." Gabby wasn't about to tell her it could

be just a few hours or as long as twenty-four or more. If Cameron was stressing now, that would probably send her into a panic. "I'm going to check your cervix to see how much it's thinning and dilating, which may give us a clue how far along you are."

"Okay, but I want an epidural, because it already hurts a lot! So please call whoever does that right away. Unless Rafael will do that himself?"

"Epidurals are done by an anesthesiologist. We'll let Dr. Moreno decide when that should happen." Since he'd wanted to be in charge, Gabby was more than happy to pass the epidural discussion on to him.

It seemed Gabby had barely plumped Cameron's pillows a third time and gotten ice for her to suck on when Rafael Moreno strode into the room as if he owned the place. All tall and powerful and regal, his mere presence seemed to electrify the air. His gaze trapped hers, and everything in the room seemed to fade away except for that intense connection. Suddenly she felt a little unsteady on her feet, but that was probably sheer exhaustion.

"Thank God you're here, Rafael!"

Cameron's voice snapped her back to reality. *Focus on your job and patient, silly, not the handsome prince.* Um, what had she been about to do just then? "Hello, Dr. Moreno. As I told you, Cameron's had PPROM. I was about to check her cervical thinning and dilation."

"What's PPROM?" Cameron sounded alarmed, and Gabby gave her a pat.

"Sorry, I was talking to the doctor. It's just an acronym for preterm premature rupture of membranes, which just means your waters broke before baby is full term."

"Let's check how far along you are, Cameron, okay?" he asked. Rafael donned gloves and began the internal exam, smiling at their patient and asking questions as he did. Somehow he managed to have her smiling back and laughing at a few of his remarks, and Gabby had to grudgingly admit he had a wonderful bedside manner, obviously used to dealing with even the most nervous and difficult kinds of patients.

When he finished the exam he snapped off his gloves and seemed to take a moment to think of how he wanted to present his findings. "Your special little one is, as we know, very anxious to arrive. You are already dilated to six centimeters, which is a bit surprising for a first baby, though of course your *bebé* has been impatient for some time, hasn't she?"

Gabby stared at him in surprise and had to bite her tongue to keep from blurting out something like *You're kidding!* Six centimeters was way further along than she'd expected, and she had to admit she was glad Rafael was already there, or she would have been concerned that he might not get to the clinic in time, which would have worried Cameron at a time she didn't need more worries.

"Oh, my Lord, then I need to get an epidural right now, don't I?" The blue eyes staring at Rafael quickly became panicky as she apparently experienced a contraction. Panting for a moment, she leaned forward to grab his hand. "I hate pain. You can make sure I don't have any more pain, right? Fix that for me, please."

So used to addressing laboring mother's worries, Gabby opened her mouth before realizing Cameron had asked Rafael, not her. And much as it rankled a bit, since she was used to either delivering babies on her own or being part of a team with the obstetrician, she managed to let him answer instead.

"I have already spoken to the anesthesiologist, as I know you want to be as comfortable as possible," he said in that soothing voice that was also, damn it, incredibly sexy.

"Now that we know you're dilated enough to receive the pain relief, we'll get the anesthesiologist here pronto."

He turned the power of his smile on Gabby, and she had to admit to a warmth filling her chest that he'd included her with the "we" word. Though why she should care if he did or didn't give her that lip service, she had no clue.

"Gabriella, would you please ask Dr. Smith to come now?"

"Yes, Dr. Moreno."

"Please, call me Rafael. You and Cameron and I are all friends trusting one another here to bring baby into the world, yes?"

"Um, yes." No. Not friends. Colleagues. Co-workers. But that simple word—*friends*—made her chest feel warmer even as it contracted with pain as she went to phone the doctor. Her last relationship had taught her that counting on true friendship and closeness with a man was a mistake. That trust was a mirage. An elusive shimmer of light that could disintegrate and disappear in an instant when times got tough.

Briefly closing her eyes, she willed away the hurt, stuffing it down into the deep, dark corner where it usually resided, until unexpected moments like this dragged it to the surface. But this moment wasn't about her past. This moment was about helping a mother who would soon hold a new life in her arms, a precious child she obviously wanted with all her heart.

Tears unexpectedly stung her eyes, and she angrily swiped them aside. She delivered babies for a living, and usually felt nothing but joy for the new parents, new families. So what was it about this moment, this delivery that was bringing memories to the surface that were better left behind?

The question made her wonder if, somehow, some way,

for some bizarre reason, it was Rafael's presence that was making her feel so strange. But, of course, that made no sense. She didn't even know him. Didn't want to.

She kept her life simple. Worked a lot of hours, taking on as many double shifts as possible. Went out with friends occasionally, but that was pretty much it. Could it be that after such a long time of keeping to herself, being around an exceptionally attractive man, annoying or not, had her neglected hormones all charged up or something?

Yes. That had to be it. And knowing that was all it was helped her get her equilibrium back. Time to quit thinking and remembering and start working. She quickly contacted the anesthesiologist, then headed back to Cameron's room.

"You checked Cameron for her group B beta strep culture, yes?" Rafael asked from his position by Cameron's bedside, holding her hand the way she would have, in a way she couldn't remember ever seeing an OB interact with a patient.

"I did. Status was uncertain, so I gave her a second dose of antibiotics in case it's an issue."

"Good." He nodded and stood, and Gabby found herself fixated on the way his broad shoulders and chest filled out his scrubs, how his tanned forearms looked more like they belonged to an athlete than a man who caught babies for a living. Thankfully, her inappropriate perusal was interrupted as Dr. Smith strode in. Face heating, she turned away, hoping to heck no one had noticed her staring.

The doctors shook hands before the anesthesiologist introduced himself to their patient. "Cameron, I promise I'm not going far, just giving Dr. Smith and Gabriella some room," Rafael said. "I'm sure Dr. Smith will take good care of you, and of course you are in Gabriella's excellent hands as well. See you shortly, okay?"

And Gabby sure as heck needed a little space and a

breather from Rafael Moreno. She did her darnedest to focus on only Cameron, but as he walked by her she found it impossible to not be aware of the pull of his green eyes, the angular shape of his smooth, golden features, and the sheer masculine force of his presence.

To cover up her confusion over this odd discomfort, she nearly asked tartly if it was okay for her to do an internal exam now, but resisted the urge. She was pretty certain that antagonizing him would just ratchet up this peculiar sizzle between them, and whether it was animosity or something else, Gabby wasn't sure anymore.

Rafael left her to monitor Cameron's labor progress and take care of her, checking in only occasionally, which Gabby was glad about on more than one level. She couldn't deny feeling pleased that he'd obviously come to trust she knew what she was doing, then inwardly scolded herself for that. He should have assumed she was competent at her job, not the other way around, especially knowing James Rothsberg and what he demanded of everyone who worked at the clinic he'd founded.

Rafael not hovering around the room, monitoring everything she did, was another good thing, though why she kept finding him so distracting she had no idea. The man was an expert at turning his charm on and off at will.

"How long is this going to take, for heaven's sake? I thought she was coming soon." Cameron's voice had gotten steadily more frustrated as her contractions got closer together, and Gabby prayed for both their sakes she was close to being ready to push.

"Your baby has a mind of her own already, Cameron, doesn't she?" she said, keeping her voice light. "First she's in a hurry, then she takes her time." A bit like her mother. "The good news is her heart rate looks perfect on the monitor. Let me check your dilation again. Looks like the epidural is keeping you comfortable, isn't it?"

"I guess. If you can call starving to death comfortable." Cameron sighed dramatically as she crunched another of the tiny round ice cubes Gabby had replaced in her cup three times now. "You'd think that with modern medicine, giving birth could be completely pain-free."

"A few decades back, women were given morphine and scopolamine to put them into a twilight sleep. They'd hallucinate, then not remember the birth at all afterwards. I don't know about you, but I'd want to remember forever the moment my baby arrived in this world."

It wasn't the kind of memory she'd wish on anyone, but it was still hers. To rail against, to shrink from, to cherish.

She could see him as clearly as if he were even now in her arms. Stillborn. One simple word that perfectly described a lifeless infant.

Motionless. Quiet. Angelic and beautiful.

Every detail of that day was burned into her very soul. And she prayed it wasn't a memory Cameron would ever have to share.

"I suppose," Cameron said grudgingly. "So, how many centimeters dilated am I?"

Grateful for the distraction, Gabby checked and was surprised and more than happy at what she found. "Guess what? You're at ten centimeters and fully effaced. Time for baby to come into the world."

"Oh, my gosh—really? Don't you need to call Rafael? What if she comes out before he gets here?"

Gabby wanted to remind Cameron that she was a qualified midwife, fully capable of delivering a baby on her own, but managed to keep her mouth shut. Besides, she'd be lying if she didn't admit she kind of wanted to see Rafael at work. "I'll give him a call right now."

"No need. I'm here," a deep voice said, and Gabby glanced up to see Rafael looking relaxed yet wired, obviously ready to get to work. "I had a feeling your little *bebé* had finally made up her mind."

"That's because you and I are *simpatico*, don't you think? How much longer?"

"Time to be the strong woman you are and get pushing with the next contraction, *sí*?"

Cameron nodded, and Gabby was surprised at how quickly her next contraction came. Rafael was calmly encouraging as long minutes passed, stretching into a half hour, with their patient becoming more frustrated and impatient with each push.

"My friend had her baby sucked out with something. Can't you just do that?" she gasped.

"Ah, 'sucked out.' That's a funny way to put it, though accurate, I suppose." Across their patient, his amused eyes met Gabby's and she felt her lips curving. "But it is not a good idea to use the vacuum on a premature infant, and you're doing well. Isn't she, Gabriella?"

"Wonderful. Just remember to breathe with the next push, okay?" She reached for Cameron's hand, stroking it. "Puff, puff, puff. In and out. Tuck down your chin when you push to give it some extra oomph, okay?"

"Extra oomph." Rafael's laughing eyes met hers again. "You Americans use amusing words. I must take notes."

"Well, do it some other time," Cameron said tartly. "I'm more interested in getting this baby out than helping you write a thesaurus of American words."

"Just trying to distract you from your hard work, Cameron. Another push now, please."

He turned those green eyes back to their patient and

Gabby realized she'd been briefly mesmerized—again—by that gaze. She glanced at the monitor wrapped around Cameron's belly as she pushed again, and the reading jerked her mind back to work. "Fetal monitor is showing a decreased variability, Dr. Moreno."

He glanced at it, too, and his expression turned serious. "Keep an eye on it during the next contractions."

"What? What does that mean? Is something wrong?" Cameron nearly moaned the questions as she pushed again.

"Baby's heartbeat is a little flat. But that may just mean she's sleeping."

"Sleeping? How could she possibly be sleeping when she's about to be born?"

"She's warm and cozy inside her mama, and also tiny because she is early. So sleeping is a possibility, though I agree it seems odd that babies sometimes are sleep before being born, doesn't it?"

His eyes met Gabby's, and she read the message in their serious depths. He wanted her to pay close attention to the monitor, and she gave him a small nod. She pressed the intercom around her neck as she watched the baby's heartbeat. "I'll give Neonatal a quick call to get them here and ready."

As Gabby spoke soothingly and encouragingly, Rafael interrupted. "Baby's head is crowning, Cameron! Not too much longer now. You are doing such a good job."

"Yes, a few more good pushes and hopefully she'll be here! Tuck that chin in again and give us another push, okay?" Gabby wiped Cameron's forehead at the same time she glanced again at the monitor and froze for an instant. "Heart rate's flat on the monitor, Dr. Moreno."

"Stop pushing, Cameron," he said in a sharp tone.

"Stop?" The woman looked at him, her tired eyes wide.

"What do you mean? I thought you said her head was crowning!"

"The cord is around her neck. I need to get it off before she can arrive."

CHAPTER THREE

CAMERON LET OUT a long cry full of dismay and fear, and Gabby held her hand tighter. "Hang in there, Cameron. Rafael's getting his fingers under the cord."

Gabby kept her voice calm and quiet but her chest squeezed hard when she saw the cord wasn't just around the baby's neck, it was wrapped round a full three times between her collarbone and her tiny chin. Dear God, this was the last thing a preterm newborn already bound to be in distress should go through.

Throat tight, she watched Rafael carefully wiggle his fingers between the cord and the baby's neck. Gabby was pretty sure she didn't breathe at all as the long, tense seconds passed while he worked gently to loosen it.

"What's happening?" Cameron asked in a high-pitched voice. "Is…is she okay? Oh, God."

"Working on it. Hold on."

His fingers finally loosened the cord enough to slip it over the baby's head, and air spilled from Gabby's lungs in a relieved whoosh. "Cord's clear now, Cameron. Get ready."

"Looks like she's been doing synchronized swimming in there to get so tangled up," Rafael said as he flashed a quick grin.

How he managed to look so completely collected,

Gabby wasn't sure, and hoped she always exuded the same calm confidence whenever she had to deal with a tricky situation. "Rafael has her head and shoulders now. One more big push, okay?"

"Good. Perfect. And…here she is!" Rafael had the infant in his hands, his dazzling smile lighting up the room as he held her. "You were *magnifico*! *Bravo!*"

Gabby quickly laid a towel on Cameron's chest so Rafael could briefly place the baby there for Cameron to see her for just a moment as the neonatal team swooped into the room. Cameron looked down at the tiny little face, not a good color yet, still too purple, but Gabby's heart lifted when she saw the infant was already pinking up.

"My sweet precious," Cameron whispered. Two wide eyes stared back at her, and the new mother promptly burst into noisy tears that pulled hard at Gabby's heart. "I love you so much. Please be okay. Please be healthy and normal and not damaged because I didn't eat enough and worked too much and squeezed my belts too tight when you were growing. Worrying about myself instead of you. Please, Skye. Please be the perfect angel I dreamed you would be."

Skye. Cameron had airily claimed she had no idea what she'd name her baby, but Gabby had always suspected she just hadn't been ready to share it. And as she looked at the tiny, scrawny baby's blue eyes, she got choked up herself, knowing so well the guilt Cameron felt. Worries she hadn't shared with Gabby. And she understood. Because she, too, didn't share her guilt with anyone.

Skye was exactly the right choice for the new life in front of her. A pure and precious gift, like any baby was to its mother. Even those who never had their chance to grow up.

"Skye is a beautiful name." Gabby gently wiped Cameron's perspiring brow once more, thinking how the woman looked more beautiful at that moment than all the times her makeup was immaculate and her hair perfectly done by her professional stylists. Having worked so hard to bring her baby into the world, she looked vulnerable and scared and more like a real person than Gabby had ever seen her—not at all the ultra-confident screen persona and diva actress she projected to the world most of the time.

For a moment, she let herself watch a little longer. To see Skye whisked to the heat lamp by the neonatal team, a bulb suction quickly clearing her nose before the small oxygen mask was placed over her head. To marvel at the little body being cleaned up and swaddled tight as Gabby would have done if the baby hadn't had the stress of the cord scare added to her being so premature.

Then she didn't want to watch anymore. She turned to focus back on Cameron and caught Rafael's eye. An eye that seemed to be searching right into her very soul, seeing far too much, and she quickly turned away from that unnerving green gaze.

"She is so beautiful, Cameron," she said, wishing her voice wasn't tight with unshed tears. "Hard work bringing her into the world, I know. But now she's here, you can spoil her rotten."

"Yes," Cameron said in a wobbly voice as she watched the neonatal team take Skye from the room to the NICU. "Yes, I plan to do just that."

"You did great," Rafael said. "I'm not surprised that the real Cameron Fontaine is even more of a warrior than the parts you play." The smile he gave the actress looked so sincere, Gabby wasn't sure if he meant it or if he was as good an actor as their patient.

"Thank you," Cameron said, but without the preening

she usually responded with when given a compliment. "But what if she's not all right?"

"No worries until we have to worry, right? What is it you Americans say? Don't borrow trouble?" Another flash of white teeth. "I will get you fixed up, then we'll see if we can sneak you in to see your *bebé*, and ask the doctors how she is doing. Okay?"

Cameron simply nodded, her lip trembling, and Gabby wanted to distract her from her worries. Maybe distract herself a little too. "You must be hungry after all that hard work. How about I get you a bite to eat? What sounds good?"

"Just crackers or something. And maybe juice. Do you have orange juice?"

"You want it, we've got it." Which was pretty much true, as the clinic had more different kinds of food and drinks to offer patients than the biggest restaurant in L.A.

Trying to think about food instead of everything else occupying her mind, Gabby could hear Rafael's deep voice chatting with Cameron as she left the room. She'd already seen he was good with patients, seeming to know when they needed to be firmly told what to do, and when they needed comfort or distraction instead. And, yes, she'd also seen he wasn't *all* arrogant, full of himself princely fluff. That might be a part of him, but there was no denying he was an excellent medical doctor too.

Which, dang it, were all unfortunate realizations, because it had been much easier to ignore the man's overwhelming mojo when she'd thought he was just a handsome, royal jerk.

She concentrated on figuring out what might appeal to Cameron, to focus on *work*, which was how she always coped when something happened to yank her back in time. But how could she deny that concentrating on

Rafael Moreno for a moment instead was an awfully appealing distraction?

Promising herself she wouldn't look at said distraction as she walked back to the room with a tray, she stopped dead in the doorway. For one heart-stopping moment she thought Rafael and Cameron were in an embrace, and she stared as a horrifying thought followed. Which was that the man was taking advantage of his beautiful patient at a vulnerable time.

Then her heart jerkily started up again when she realized that Cameron was sobbing, tears streaking down her cheeks as she rested her head against Rafael's broad shoulder, her hands clutching his scrub shirt. That his large hand gently stroking her damp hair back from her face was meant to comfort and soothe. Soft and beautiful Spanish words were coming from his beautifully shaped lips, and though Gabby's knowledge of the language wasn't as good as it should have been, she recognized them as words of praise and reassurance.

Oh. My. In her years as a midwife, working with doctors of all kinds, she'd seen many who were wonderful with patients. But this? This was something entirely new to her experience. This man was one lethal combination of excellent medical skill, patient care, and soothing empathy, with movie-star good looks on top of it all.

A sudden vision of his big, tanned hand pushing back her own hair, cupping her jaw before lowering those sensual lips to hers nearly stopped her breath. At that moment, he seemed to realize she'd come just inside the door and looked up. Still holding Cameron, patting her shoulder, his attention somehow seemed to be one hundred percent on Gabby as his eyes met hers. His lips curved in a slow smile, and his head inclined toward her ever so slightly in a subtle but obvious compliment. Giving her his respect and silent kudos that he thought she'd done a good job.

Somehow she managed to break that mesmerizing eye contact, breathe, and get her feet moving to the side of the bed. Her heart pounded hard in her ears, but thank heavens he couldn't hear it. Could he?

She shook her head at herself and tried to keep her attention on just Cameron, but that was nearly impossible since her face was buried in Rafael's neck, and she was hanging on to him like a barnacle to a rock. "I brought you a few different things to eat." Other than Rafael. Gabby found herself momentarily distracted, wondering how, exactly, his neck smelled. Tasted. She'd bet pretty darned good on both counts. "Try a few, and if you think of something else you'd like to have, I'll be happy to get it for you."

Cameron slowly eased away from Rafael, her hands releasing his scrub shirt to swipe at the tears on her face. Rafael reached for a tissue to hand her and she gave him a grateful smile. "Thank you. Both of you. You've been just wonderful to me through all this, and I really, truly appreciate it."

"It has been a privilege to be a part of it, Ms. Fontaine." Rafael stood from his position by the bed. "I need to make a few notes and talk to the pediatrician about when we can see *bebé*. I'll be right back."

Gabby watched Cameron dig into her food with surprising gusto, considering how emotional she'd been a moment ago, and how she'd mostly picked at her food before then. "I'm glad you're eating. It'll help you get your strength back faster."

"I'd thought I'd felt starved before, all the times I'd hardly eaten, trying to stay skinny to get into my costumes. But this time I'm honest to goodness famished!"

"Anything else you want, just let me know."

“I want to see Skye.” She put the fork down and tears welled in her eyes again. “Rafael said he’d get me there as soon as possible.”

“I’m sure they’ll let you go to see her very soon. They know how important it is for a new mother to be with her baby.”

“I hope so.” Cameron sighed, and this time it sounded less worried and more dreamy. “Rafael’s the sweetest, isn’t he? Just wonderful. Gorgeous. Edible.”

Edible? Apparently, Gabby wasn’t the only one who’d had that passing thought. Then immediately had a vision of Cameron nibbling on the man’s sexy lips. Lips she couldn’t deny any woman would like a taste of.

Was Cameron planning on making a play for him once she was out of the hospital? Gabby had to wonder if he’d be more than happy to take the A-list actress up on anything she might offer. Then again, she’d just given birth, so they wouldn’t…

She drew herself up short and stuffed down those ridiculous and plain awful thoughts. What in the world would make her start thinking about the sex lives of either one was beyond her. She didn’t do relationships anymore. Sex either, and maybe that was why it had come to mind at all. It had been a long time and, hey, she was only human, right? What warm-blooded woman wouldn’t think about sex at least briefly when sharing the same air as Rafael Moreno?

Thankfully, the man entered the room at that moment, so she didn’t have to respond to Cameron’s comment. Or maybe she wasn’t thankful, because her wayward thoughts sent her gaze straight to his lips and, yes, she couldn’t deny they looked very edible indeed. She quickly moved her attention to the bronze color of his throat visible in the V of his scrubs, then on to the broad, powerful chest stretching his scrub shirt taut.

His eyes met hers with something unnerving glimmering in that startling green, and she had that *can't breathe* feeling again. Lord, did he know, somehow, she'd been thinking about his nibble-worthy lips?

"Has our patient had a bite to eat?" he asked in a low, rumbling voice meant for Gabby's ears only. Also meant to make women swoon, if the shivers currently skittering down Gabby's spine were any indication.

"Um, yes." Gabby cleared her throat. "Did NICU say she could see Skye now?"

"*Sí.* They've given us the green light, and transport is coming to get her as we speak." He turned to smile at Cameron, speaking louder now. "Ready to see your beautiful girl now?"

"Yes, I'm so ready!" Cameron shoved aside her food. "Is she okay? Is she going to be fine?"

"Be prepared that she is in an incubator, being given extra-special care. So don't be scared when you see that a few tubes are attached to her. The neonatal specialist will talk with you, but I can tell you she is optimistic."

Gabby noted that he stopped short of committing to the baby being fine, which was wise, considering how premature Skye was and the multiple wraps of the umbilical cord around her little neck. He moved to the bed to pat Cameron on the shoulder again, leaving his backside turned to Gabby's view. A tight, prime backside that filled out his scrubs all too well. Not that she was looking.

"Well, what's taking them so long to come get me so I can see her?"

Gabby hadn't thought she'd ever welcome Cameron's demanding tone, but this time she was glad to hear it. Far preferable to how upset and vulnerable-sounding she'd been earlier.

As if her imperious voice had commanded it, transport arrived seconds later. Gabby moved to help Cameron down from the bed into the wheelchair, but to her astonishment Rafael simply lifted their patient up and gently deposited her in it, as though she weighed little more than her newborn.

"Are you coming with me, Rafael?" Cameron asked, clutching his arm. Her blue eyes were wide and imploring, and her lips were quivering again. Gabby had spent a lot of hours with Cameron, and had a sneaking suspicion the woman was pulling out her acting skills.

Curious to see how Rafael would react, Gabby nonchalantly glanced at him out of the corner of her eye.

"I will join you as soon as Gabriella and I finish up here."

It must have been Cameron's exhaustion that had her simply nodding instead of arguing. An evil part of Gabby that she hadn't even known was inside her had her smiling, wondering how Cameron would react if she said, *I'll join you and Rafael as soon as possible too!*

Then felt horribly guilty about that when Cameron reached for her hand, holding it until the transport guy had to stop wheeling her. "You've been so wonderful in every way, taking care of me and my little Skye long before she was born, and I'm so grateful. I hope you know that."

"Oh, Cameron." The sweet words touched her, especially coming from someone who'd seemed oblivious to many of Gabby's ministrations throughout these long hours. "It's been my pleasure and honor. And of course I'll be checking on you and Skye while you're still here at the clinic."

Cameron squeezed her hand, and she squeezed back

just before the wheelchair moved on out of the room. She thought of the new mother seeing her baby again, touching her small body through the incubator ports, and knew exactly how overwhelming that maternal love felt. The only kind of forever love, no matter what the circumstances.

She turned to see Rafael Moreno studying her, his eyebrows twitched together questioningly. She wondered what he was seeing, and put on a bright smile. "Congratulations, Dr. Moreno! You dealt with everything very impressively. So scary that the cord was wrapped around her neck three times—I've rarely seen that. She pinked up fast, though, so I think you got it handled before she'd suffered any oxygen deprivation."

"I hope so. We'll see what the blood gases show."

"Are you worried?" The man looked oddly serious, and Gabby wondered for a second if he'd seen something more alarming than she had.

"No. I agree with you that she looks remarkably good, considering everything. But I owe you an apology."

"For what?" The intense way he was staring at her made her stomach feel strangely twisty and her skin warm and tingly. Hoping he wouldn't notice, she tried for a joke. "Telling me I'm a lousy housekeeper?"

A slight smile alleviated some of the ultra-seriousness from his face. "Yes. And also that I implied you were incompetent."

"Less of an implication than a statement, Dr. Moreno. I believe you said the condition of the room was obvious evidence you had to take control of my ward and care of my patient."

"And I was wrong. Something that rarely happens." His smile grew wider. "I have seen you are excellent at what you do, both with patient care and medical care. I was glad to have you working with me today, keeping me informed of the variables on the monitor, which had me looking for complications when baby's head had barely crowned. Cameron and Skye have much to thank you for."

"Well." What was it about this man that sent her breathing haywire with a simple compliment? Or was it more the way those green eyes caught and held hers? "I appreciate you saying that. And I've seen you are an excellent doctor."

And wasn't standing there giving one another kudos beyond awkward? Gabby quickly turned to tidy the room. "I'd better get to that housekeeping before you report me to James," she said lightly, hoping to get back the equilibrium he seemed to throw out of whack every time she was near him.

"What I will report to James is that you are exceptional at dealing with patients like Cameron Fontaine. He did well to hire someone like you for a clinic catering to the rich and famous."

A club he doubtless belonged to very comfortably. "Thank you again. Likewise." Fumbling with the equipment, she managed to drop the suture kit, and items skittered in every direction across the floor.

Lord. She crouched to gather everything, feeling like a teenager hanging out with the high school football star, utterly clumsy and tongue-tied. When would the man leave so she could finish and go home to finally get more than a couple of hours' sleep? Maybe then her brain would function better around Rafael Moreno, instead of strangely short-circuiting.

Then she had a complete brain freeze when he crouched next to her, his thick shoulder bumping hers as he helped her to pick things up. "Do I make you feel nervous, Gabriella? If so, I'm sorry."

The soft rumble of his voice drew her gaze to his. She couldn't move as she stared at the closeness of his lips. At the sculpted cheekbones and jaw. At the interesting gold and brown flecks within the green staring back at her. As she breathed in the scent of him—a mix of masculinity and antiseptic soap that on him smelled so sexy, her mouth went dry.

"Nervous? No, of course not."

"I think that's a lie. That needs to change, though, as it looks like we'll be working together for the foreseeable future. So we will have dinner together, and you can educate me more about how the clinic and the maternity ward run." He dropped the items onto her tray, then gently stroked his fingertip beneath her eye. "See if you can get in a short nap before your shift ends. That's at six, *sí*? I'll be back here at seven."

Before she could formulate a single response to his astonishing suggestion he was gone, leaving her to stare openmouthed after him. When she'd gathered her wits, she stood and studied herself in the mirror, twisting her lips as her finger slowly traced the skin he'd just touched. Nothing like being told, basically, that you looked like a baggy-eyed wreck.

A wreck completely unready for a dinner date with a prince.

CHAPTER FOUR

RAFAEL STUDIED THE woman sitting across from him, nearly smiling as he watched the gusto with which Gabriella attacked her meal. No Hollywood starlet starving herself here, or one of the many jet-setting socialites he knew who ate as little as possible to save their calories for a martini or three. Not that she wasn't every bit as beautiful as those kinds of women, just harder working, spunky, and no-nonsense. Far more down to earth than the women he usually dated.

How had he never noticed the appeal of a woman like Gabriella?

"I trust that your dinner was tasty enough to overcome your doubts about sharing it with me?" he asked.

"I'm sure you've noticed that I'm practically licking my fork, and it's so yummy I'm not even embarrassed about that. So you know the answer is yes."

"Good. James recommended this restaurant, and I'm happy it lives up to its billing. And also happy that I now know the best way to persuade you is through your stomach."

"As opposed to your overbearing insults of the past?" The twinkle in her light brown eyes belied the words, which he hoped meant they'd sent their first impressions of one another into the past. "And the recent one too. And here I thought you were supposed to be a suave sophisticate with a vast knowledge of women."

"What makes you think I'm not?"

"No smart man wanting a woman to go on a dinner date tells her she should take a nap first because she has bags under her eyes. Then at dinner implies she's making a pig of herself."

He had to laugh. "I apologize profusely if that was how my words came across. Even after several long days of work, you still look amazingly beautiful. And as for the pig part, if that is you, it's now my favorite type of creature. Watching you take pleasure in your dinner has made mine that much more enjoyable."

Even in the candlelight he could see her luminous skin turn pink, which was something else attractive about her. He couldn't think of another woman he knew who would blush at a simple compliment.

"Thank you. For the dinner and the flattery. Both of which have me wondering why you invited me here tonight. What exactly are you wanting from me?"

What did he want from her? He'd thought it was simply a cordial working relationship, learning from her the nuances of how The Hollywood Hills Clinic worked. But her words suddenly had him thinking about something entirely different, and his body stirred with a surge of testosterone.

There had to be legions of men who reacted to her the same way. He had to wonder if she had a man in her life. If she didn't that would be surprising, but perhaps he'd caught her between boyfriends. Except he couldn't be "catching" her at all, since the whole reason he was in L.A. was to steer clear of women and keep his face out of the papers until the heat from his parents cooled off. Their attitudes annoyed the hell out of him, but he still cared about them.

It was probably part of his duties as a son to avoid giving either one of them apoplexy.

"All I want is for us to work well together, the way we did with Cameron this afternoon. And to learn a little about the clinic from you." He stuffed down the wayward thoughts pushing him to ask about her personal life and sent her a smile he hoped was blandly professional. "Tell me why you became a midwife and where you trained."

"I'm from a family of several generations of midwives, which isn't as common here in the U.S. as in some other countries. I always knew that was what I wanted to do. Trained at a nursing school, then a midwifery program near Seattle, which is where I'm from."

"And you came here after training?"

"No. I worked at a private midwifery unit there for quite a while. Came here two years ago."

Was he imagining the shuttering of her eyes? That the relaxed smile on her face just moments ago had stiffened into something else? "Was it the appeal of working with famous people that drew you here?" He didn't think so—she just didn't seem like the type to care about that, but it wasn't as though he really knew her.

"No. They'd approached me a few years before I came, then I…decided I wanted a change, and let them know I was available. How about you?" Her brown eyes held something—sadness maybe?—along with a clear determination to change the subject. "I have to admit it's surprising to me that someone born a prince would decide to become a doctor."

"Unless that prince is the second born. My parents saw my role within the kingdom as leading charity work, and while that's worthwhile, I felt there were plenty of others who would happily take on that job. I wanted a career helping people in my own way, and my parents never understood that. Also, they got very annoyed the times I ducked out of various superficial royal duties."

"What kind of royal duties?"

"Number one would be cutting a ribbon for the grand opening of a museum or concert hall or school. I was taught from a young age how to keep my scissors sharp."

He was glad she laughed at his joke, but there was a nugget of truth to it. His parents couldn't fathom why he'd become a doctor, and Gabriella no doubt wouldn't be able to understand that attitude, since she was a medical professional too. God knew, he'd spent years trying to figure out why they disapproved of him and his choices, and he had finally given up worrying about it.

"Since you could be anything you wanted to be, how did you decide to go into medicine?"

"From the time I was small, I was fascinated with anatomy, dissecting worms and frogs with my tutors. Later, I insisted on studying the animals butchered on our land to feed the royal household and its guests, much to my mother's horror."

Her dazzling, real smile came back, lighting the darkness of their corner table. "I can imagine that might be alarming. Did she think you might grow up to be an axe murderer?"

"Probably. Or, worse, a livestock farmer. Facing the options of her son's occupation being murderer, farmer, or doctor, she reluctantly accepted the latter."

"A wise woman. So how did you decide to become an OB/GYN? Or is that something personal I don't want to know?"

Her soft laughter had him staring at her mouth, and he wished that, just once, he could taste it. Just to see if it was as soft and sweet as it looked like it would be. "My reputation isn't as bad as you might have heard, so it's not the reason you're thinking. You of all people should know the amazement and joy of assisting a new life. I had that experience totally by accident, when I was visiting a sheikh friend whose wife went into labor unexpectedly. Being there with my friend and his wife to bring their newborn into the world was such an amazing experience, I knew that was what I wanted to do."

"That's a wonderful story. You could have just spent your life traveling the world in search of fun, but instead want to make a difference in people's lives. I really respect that."

The way her eyes shined at him in genuine admiration had him nearly confessing to the many failings he was all too guilty of, but letting her think he was wonderful was far preferable. "I went to medical school with James Rothsberg. We learned what hard work and drive could accomplish, no matter which world you're born into." Especially when that world always looked to find the worst in you, instead of the best. Set examples he had no interest in following, like tethering yourself to a permanent marital relationship for no reason other than convenience.

Her expression turned even more admiring, and as she opened her mouth to ask another question he realized he'd already said too much in terms of true confessions for the night. "Would you care for coffee? How about a look at the dessert menu? I'm guessing you're still not quite full."

"Again, your comment could be interpreted as an insult instead of an offer. But I'll let it slide, since I did put teeth marks on my spoon."

"And the price of a replacement spoon will doubtless be added to the bill, but just this once I'll take care of it. So, dessert?"

"No, thank you." Her fingertips covered a small yawn that morphed into a big one, until she laughed about it.

And what was more adorable than a woman who could poke fun at herself? "I'm sorry, but I'm really, really tired. Worked several double shifts, then stayed with Cameron for the past two days. And she needed a thing or two over all those hours that interrupted my dozing."

"I can only imagine," he said dryly, picturing Cameron wanting any number of luxuries as she'd lain in that bed. "And can also imagine you giving her the best of care, regardless of the way it was requested."

"Do I deserve all that credit if I was sometimes secretly irritated in the midst of it?" Her grin was interrupted by another yawn, this one audible. "Oh, my gosh, I'm so sorry. I need to get home to sleep."

"Yes, you do." He quickly scribbled on the check and rose to take her elbow, helping her from the chair to guide her out the door. It was apparent she'd been pushing herself past her limit for days, and he was struck with a sudden, surprising desire to take care of her. A wish that he was close enough to her to have the right to tuck her into bed for a long, well-deserved rest.

But he wasn't and couldn't be. Problem was, only moments after she settled into the leather seat of his car, she fell fast asleep.

So what was he supposed to do now? He drove toward the clinic, the original plan being to drop her off so she could drive her car to her own home. If he had any idea where that was, he would simply drive her there himself. But he didn't have a clue if she lived east or west or north or south of the clinic.

He glanced at her for the tenth time, noting the way the peach-blonde fire of her hair had slipped across her face. Tangling in her long lashes, the silken strands caressed her cheekbones and lay across the corner of her lush lips. Pulling to a stop in the clinic lot, he reached over to gently smooth her hair back, letting his fingers linger on the softness of both her cheek and hair.

"Gabriella? Gabby?" For the first time he used her nickname and found he much preferred her given name, which he'd enjoyed the sound of the moment it had first rolled off his tongue. *Gabriella.* It suited her. Beautiful and feminine. Strong and intelligent. "Wake up. Do you want me to take you home, instead of you driving there? Where do you live?"

No response at all. Just the sound of gentle breathing through slightly parted lips. He did the usual things. Shook her slender shoulder. Asked the same questions louder. And when she still slept like an angel, he made up his mind.

Instead of rousing her enough to get her in her car to drive home, possibly still dangerously half-asleep, he'd take her to his house and tuck her into one of the comfortable guest suites. That way, she'd be sure to get the long sleep she obviously desperately needed. After all, it was his fault she wasn't already in bed, having insisted she dine with him tonight.

Hopefully the paparazzi weren't lurking around the house he was renting. He was pretty sure they'd only watched him the first couple of weeks after he'd arrived in L.A., then moved on to more exciting prey when he'd behaved himself.

He studied her delicate profile. Her straight nose and a slightly stubborn jaw that suited her. The appealing dip above her pretty lips, soft and sweet in sleep. Yes, getting her to his house was the best way to handle the situation. Gabriella would sleep well and be grateful in the morning, ready to tackle her day at work with her usual energy.

But, a little later, as he swung her soft, warm body into his arms, carrying her fast asleep into the house, that surge of testosterone hit him even harder than before. The feel of her sweet curves pressed against him shortened his breath and sent his heart rate into double time, and neither had anything to do with the exertion of carrying her dead weight. It was then he realized, too late, the big downside of his decision.

Gabriella would get a good night's sleep. But he had a feeling she'd be the only one in the house who did.

The sensation of silky-soft sheets and light, cozy down wrapped Gabby in a snug cocoon as her senses slowly came to consciousness. Feeling more comfortable than she'd ever felt in her life, she lay there in tranquil warmth, a small smile on her face. Feeling wonderful. Feeling indulged and pampered, but why that was, she wasn't sure.

Her palms slowly stretched across the linens, over the fluffy comforter enveloping her, eventually wrapping her arms around herself, savoring the sensation.

Where was she? Not in her little apartment. On a vacation in some exotic place? No, she hadn't been vacationing. Obviously this was some hedonistic dream and she'd be waking soon.

Somehow she managed to crack open her heavy eyelids. And realized it wasn't a dream. She really was in this ridiculously comfortable bed, but where that bed was, she had no clue.

Abruptly, her eyelids shot wide open and, heart tripping, she sat up, trying to get her eyes accustomed to the darkness. Trying to figure out whether or not her beautiful, comfortable dream was really some horrible nightmare.

And realized this was, for certain, most definitely not her bed. So whose was it? Dragging in a rattling breath, she uttered an involuntary shriek and leapt out of the bed, blindly stumbling toward the shadowy door she thought she could see across the room. Fumbling with the latch, she yanked it open, through it into freedom, only to smack right into something large looming across the threshold.

Something hard but smooth. Something warm to the touch, with a rough covering that felt like hair. Something immovable that grasped her arms, holding her. Imprisoning her.

A full-fledged scream tore from her lips. “Let me go!” She writhed to free herself from the monster, to no avail. “Let. Me. Go!”

“Good Lord, Gabriella.” The words were tense but soft as the hold on her loosened. “It’s me, Rafael. Please stop screaming. It’s all right.”

Another scream about to rip from her throat, she blinked up to see a sculpted jaw, and though the mouth above it was tightened into a thin line, they were obviously the sensually shaped lips of Rafael Moreno. Relief had her sagging against him. “Oh, my heavens. I woke up and… didn’t know where I was.” And still didn’t, and that realization brought her fully alert. “So…what in the world happened? Where am I?”

“In my home. You were sound asleep in my car. In a near coma really—I couldn’t rouse you.”

His lips had softened into a smile, and his eyes gleamed at her through the darkness. The bizarreness of the situation finally sank in, and she started to get suspicious then angry. What grown woman would fall asleep so completely she wouldn’t wake up when someone tried to, as he’d said, “rouse” her?

She realized her palms were pressed flat against his hard pectorals and soft, hair-roughened skin. Heat seemed to pump from that wide, masculine chest, enveloping her and making it hard to breathe. She yanked her hands off like she’d touched the sun, flinging them to her own chest to do a quick check of what exactly she was—or wasn’t—

wearing, then jerked out of his hold completely. Relief that she still had on the clothes she'd worn on their dinner date didn't temper the anger making her start to physically shake.

"I can't believe you brought me here, then inside your house to…to put me in bed like a child. Why would you do that? I thought for a minute you must have drugged me or something. And…and taken advantage of me."

Infuriatingly, instead of looking contrite or insulted, his arrogantly amused smile widened. "Believe me, *belleza*, I don't have to drug women for them to wish to come home with me, nor do I have to take advantage of them. They are, instead, quite happy to take advantage of me."

She parted her lips to say something caustic in response, but nothing came out. Because she'd just realized he stood there not only shirtless but was wearing only boxers on his bottom half. Boxers that hung low on his hips, and even in the darkness she could see the ripples of muscles across his middle and the big, sculpted quadriceps of his legs beneath the hem that stopped well above his mid-thigh.

It had been a long time since she'd been with a man. And never one with so much potent masculine appeal, it should be illegal. She sucked in a breath so she could finally talk, but unfortunately brought his scent inside her nose and nearly felt dizzy from it. "Well, I'm not one of them."

"Sadly, I'm aware of that. In fact, you've crushed my ego. Never have I had a woman fall asleep in my company unless it was after a long night of making love."

The rumble of his voice combined with his deliciously drawling accent and his inappropriate mention of love-making sent shivers across her skin. Or maybe she was just cold, having left the comfortable bed and the heat of his body. A peculiar tension curled through her body, and she had an almost irresistible urge to snuggle up against that firm, warm chest, imagining how good it would feel against her.

Which was ridiculous. The man had all but kidnapped her. "I doubt if anything could crush your ego, Dr. Moreno. But now that I've woken from my *coma*, I'd appreciate it if you'd take me home."

"If you insist." The polite inclination of his head was regal, despite the fact he stood there practically naked. "But it's four a.m. and I, for one, would like to get a few more hours of sleep before work. Surely it would be best for both of us to go back to bed for a few hours."

Back to bed. What in the world was wrong with her that his words made her think of something very different from sleep? Involuntarily, a slightly hysterical giggle left her lips.

"Something amusing?"

"Just that I was thinking that, since you're a prince, you should have tried kissing me when I was asleep. I wonder if that would have worked, like in the fairy tales?"

Lord, she must be delirious. Appalled that she'd blurted her thought out loud, the feeling faded as their eyes met. His seemed to blaze at the same time his lids lowered in a look that made her quiver. "Excellent question, *bella*. Next time, I'll try that to find out, hmm?"

"There won't be a next time. But I guess you're right about it being silly to go home right now." She gulped, searching for her common sense. Time to shut down this sensual back and forth between them that she had a feeling could easily get out of control. "I'll just get back to sleep and we can leave for work in the morning. I always keep extra clothes there, anyway."

He inclined his head again. "*Bueno.* We will leave here at eight. Sleep well."

And then he was gone, taking all that heat and testosterone that had shimmered in the room with him.

Gabby shoved her fingers through her hair with a sigh and sank back into the bed, pulling the covers to her chin. She should be glad the bizarre interaction between her and Rafael was over with. Instead, she felt revitalized but at the same time there was an odd hollow in the pit of her stomach. A disappointment that he hadn't responded to her ridiculous remark about a prince kissing her awake with an actual kiss. And why had she said it, anyway? Probably because, unconsciously, she'd been thinking about it all evening as she'd stared across that candlelit table at his beautiful lips.

She flopped onto her side, trying to ignore the tense, letdown feeling around her heart, deciding not to make too much of it. The man was physically gorgeous enough to make any woman swoon, right? And she was a woman who hadn't felt much of anything for a man besides disillusionment in a long, long time.

CHAPTER FIVE

"READY FOR WORK?" Rafael asked, breaking the silence between them as he drove them to the clinic in the powerful car she barely remembered getting into after dinner last night, which made her blush all over again. "I trust your middle-of-the-night awakening didn't interfere too much with the sleep you obviously needed."

"No, thank you. I slept well." Which was a total lie. She hadn't gotten a wink after he'd left her room, imagining how awkward it would be in his house together in the morning and on the way to work. And awkward was an understatement. She'd taken the world's fastest shower in the stunning bathroom attached to the room she'd slept in, wondering if the man might not be the gentleman he seemed but instead a prince who thought he had the right to walk in on her. Then, nervous and uncomfortable, she'd stood in his kitchen, nerves twitchy, clutching her purse and ready to go, while he'd sat relaxed, drinking coffee and having a croissant.

She'd steadfastly declined his invitation to join him, partly because she'd wanted to get going and partly because he'd had a vaguely amused expression on his face. Obviously he wasn't used to women wanting to dash out his door. She didn't doubt it was usually quite the opposite.

He swung out of the car, looking smooth and handsome and not even remotely tired, like she knew she unfortunately still did. She pushed open her own door, about to get out and hurry inside as fast as she could, when he appeared, holding out his hand to her, eliminating any chance of a quick escape. She tried to walk fast, but he simply kept pace with her at her side. As they walked together to the clinic's big double doors, she blushed scarlet from head to toe.

The walk of shame. This was what friends of hers had talked about in the past! Out on a date, spend the night, and show up somewhere wearing the same clothes for all the world to see. Except she hadn't even enjoyed what people would think she had, damn it. Shamed without reason.

"I'm late for work. I'll...um...see you around." She walked faster, trying to get inside and to her locker fast, praying no one had paid attention to what dress she'd worn the night before.

Rafael caught up with her. She stared straight ahead, but he dipped his head to look at her, drawing her gaze to his. To green eyes that now danced with amusement. "Are you worried people will talk, *bella*, if they see us arrive together?"

"Yes!" she hissed. "So please go wherever you need to go and goodbye."

"Not goodbye. We're seeing a patient together in twenty minutes. Until then." He reached for her hand, his eyes twinkling above it as he pressed his lips to it. She snatched it away and practically ran down the corridor toward the women's locker room. The imprint of that quick kiss still tingled on her skin, and she had a bad feeling that meant she was in for a very long day.

Freya Rothsberg, the clinic's PR guru and also James's sister, raised her eyebrows at Gabby as she tore down the hallway, and she forced herself to slow down.

"Good morning, Gabby," Freya said.

"Good morning." Was it her imagination, or was Freya's voice a little questioning? Or was she just being completely paranoid? "I…need to get into scrubs to see my first patient. Have a great day."

Finally able to hide in the locker room, Gabby flung off her dress, quickly hung it up, then got her scrubs on. Breathing a sigh of relief, she leaned against her locker door. Clearly she wasn't up for middle-of-the-night adventures, innocent or not.

Ten minutes later, she felt almost normal and composed, putting a smile on her face as she went into her patient's room. Then every ounce of composure slid away when she saw Rafael standing there, talking with the woman.

"Ah, Gabriella." His eyes met hers, and that darned twinkle still lingered, making her feel embarrassed all over again. "I hope you don't mind, but I took the liberty of seeing your patient before you arrived, as my first patient isn't here yet."

She could feel hot color rushing into her cheeks again, annoyed as all get-out at her reaction to seeing him there. Somehow she bit back the words she wanted to say, which were, *Yes, I do mind, as a matter of fact. I'm trying to stay away from you!*

"Of course not. How are you feeling, Megan?"

"Absolutely great! I was just telling Dr. Moreno that my yoga instructor is so impressed with my workouts. I mean, I'm doing every bit as much at eight months along as I did before I got pregnant."

"As long as you're feeling good when you exercise, that's very healthy for you and your baby." She made herself turn to Rafael, and the power of that green gaze nearly choked her.

"I'm sure I'll be fit enough for the minor role Daddy

has in mind for me in the film he's starting this summer. I told Rafael he should come to the set."

"Megan's father's films are among my favorite thrillers," he said. "I particularly enjoyed that scene in his last movie where one of the main guys showed up in the heroine's bedroom, and she didn't know until then that he wasn't her friend but the terrifying killer instead. Scary stuff."

The wicked glint in those green depths was both irritating and unnerving, since it sent her thoughts right back to what she'd been trying so hard not to think about. Which was the feel of his hard, warm body against hers, and how he'd looked in those boxer shorts.

"So," she said, desperately trying to change the subject, "have you examined Megan yet, Dr. Moreno?"

"I thought I'd leave that to you, along with getting her vital signs. Just wanted to introduce myself before the big day arrives."

"Surely you won't still be working here in another month, will you?" If her voice held a trace of panic, she couldn't help it. "I thought this was a brief pit stop in your life."

"I expect I will be staying a while. I'm enjoying my time in L.A. and here at The Hollywood Hills Clinic. The staff is most...interesting, and I hope to get to know everyone much better."

Gabby dropped the blood-pressure cuff on the floor, then had to take the reading twice she was so distracted by Rafael's teasing. Which she knew full well it was—for some reason, he was enjoying yanking her chain and making her blush again.

"I'm about to do your internal exam now, Megan, okay?" She turned to Rafael with a saccharine-sweet smile, hoping her narrowed eyes told him exactly how irritated she was without showing, again, how he rattled her. "So you're free to see if your patient has arrived, Dr. Moreno."

"Why do I get the feeling the boss is tossing me out on my ear?" He turned that lethal grin on Megan. "See you next time you're in. You have my contact information if you need me."

Remarkable how the minute the man was out of the room, Gabby was able to focus on her patient and her job without dropping or forgetting a single thing. Pitiful. Which meant that, if Rafael was really going to be sticking around for a while, somehow, some way she'd have to get a handle on her ridiculous, distracted hormones.

Chuckling to himself as he walked down the hallway to see his patient, Rafael reflected on how easy it was to get under Gabriella's skin, and how much fun it was. She was such a complex mix of characteristics combined in a fascinating way, all bundled up inside a beautiful, touchable package. Sweet and smart, feisty and a little shy all at the same time, he wanted to spend more time with her. Learn a lot more about what made her tick.

He might have gotten off on the wrong foot with her initially, but he knew she found him attractive now as well. Last night when he'd held her in his hands and her wide eyes had looked up at him in the dark bedroom, he'd seen the way her lips had parted; had felt her quickened breaths skating warm and fast across his skin. The rise and fall of her chest had been less about her fear and more about sexual attraction—he knew because he'd felt the same hot vibration. Then she'd tried to cover up the zing happening between them with pretend indignation. Zing that had been a two-way street—it had taken all his *won't*-power to resist the urge to pull her closer for a kiss, to see where all that heat shimmering between them might lead.

Except he'd then figuratively smacked himself with the reminder that he was supposed to be lying low in L.A. "Behaving himself," to quote his parents, and dating "appropriate" women, whatever the hell that meant. Apparently not strippers, or those whose faces graced the gossip magazines, and why any of that was a big deal, he didn't understand.

It wasn't as though a single one of them would ever get an engagement ring from him. Seeing the various loveless marriages in his family, not to mention what James's parents' relationship had been like, Rafael figured that kind of commitment would be sheer purgatory. Why in the world would he want to handcuff himself to one woman forever if he didn't have to?

Short-term handcuffing, though? Now, that he was all for. Thinking about something short, sweet and hot with Gabriella put the smile back on his face, only it quickly faded because, damn it, he couldn't let that happen, with the media and his parents breathing down his neck.

Seeing his next patient got his thoughts back on track, and as he was about to go to the nurses' station to discuss her chart, the sound of his name on the large, wall-mounted television in the patient's room stopped him in mid-step. He looked up at the screen to see what ridiculous, untrue story was being spread on the TV gossip shows now.

To his shock, the photos were of the cliffside mansion he was renting, with two people in front of it. Pictures of him carrying a sleeping Gabriella inside, then of the two of them leaving in the morning, with sensationalized questions and speculation about who Prince Rafael Moreno's late-night booty call might be this time.

Damn it to hell. What had he just said about his parents breathing down his neck? This time they'd probably be belching pure fire. He glanced at his patient and her nurse, glad they were too busy talking to pay attention to the stupid television. He wiped his suddenly sweaty hands on his lab coat, thankful the photos were distant and grainy enough that nobody would likely be able to figure out who the woman was. He hoped Gabriella didn't get wind of the story, and hoped even more that she wouldn't suffer any embarrassment from it. Already, he knew she wasn't the kind of woman who would appreciate being part of a media frenzy, which was one of several good reasons he'd been telling himself he had to keep his hands off her.

Anger surged into his veins on her behalf. The hard-working, exhausted woman couldn't even fall asleep in his car without untrue rumors being spread, and he wished he could contact the TV programmers with a vehement rebuttal, telling them to lay off.

But experience had taught him that kind of thing just inflamed the gossipmongers even more. With any luck, the hounds would back off when they couldn't figure out who she was, and the story would die a quick death.

For Gabriella's sake, and for his too, he hoped like hell that was exactly what would happen. Seeing the photos in his mind again as he strode from the room to update the charts, he nearly ran into Freya.

"Rafael." A smile played about Freya's lips and she lifted an eyebrow. "I hear your patients love you, so thanks for stepping in. Also sounds like you're very much...enjoying your time in L.A.?"

"Not as much as I'm given credit for, I can tell you that," he said, somehow keeping his voice cool and amused, even as his stomach felt a little queasy. "The story of your life and mine, isn't it?"

"Stories aren't always fiction." Her smile widened, and she walked away without another word.

Trying to get the annoying voice of the TV host out of

his head, along with the blurry images he hoped Gabriella wouldn't have to see, he concentrated on the computerized patient charts until his phone interrupted him.

Then he knew the day was going downhill even faster when he saw it was his mother, and his gut clenched with the certain knowledge that their palace spies had informed her of the latest gossip fest.

"*Buenos días,* Mother. It's wonderful to hear your voice." Or would be, if their conversation was going to be about the palace horses or her latest fundraiser or something else pleasant and benign, but he was pretty sure he wouldn't be that lucky.

"Rafael. What do your father and I have to do to make you understand your position in life? Your responsibilities? We might not have liked that you chose to do something like doctoring instead of accepting your traditional role here, but we have learned to live with it. That doesn't give you the right, though, to disregard your family's status completely and do whatever you wish! I thought the latest scandal had taught you that. You said that's why you went to L.A. for a while, to behave! And yet here you are, the subject of gossip again. When are you going to marry a nice girl and be done with this? When—?"

"Mother." He'd gritted his teeth and held the phone from his ear during her long diatribe, but finally managed to cut her off when she took a breath. "If you're talking about the stupid TV news, I can assure you it's nothing. I'm working for a time in James's clinic, and a co-worker and I had work to discuss. She fell asleep and…" This time he cut himself off. Why the hell should he have to defend himself to anyone, including his mother, about something completely innocent? Was it his fault he'd been second born into a royal family, and because of that was a chronic disappointment and annoyance to his parents? His fault that the paparazzi liked to stalk him? As for getting married, she might as well save her breath, because that was never going to happen. "You know, I'm done with this conversation. Is there something else you'd like to talk about?"

"We need to get this ironed out first. If you—"

"Goodbye, Mother. Call me if you want to talk about something besides how much my being a doctor and a heathen embarrasses you."

Under normal circumstances, he would have felt bad hanging up on his mother, even when she was scolding him. But this subject had been beaten to death for months, and he'd moved here to escape the gossip his parents despised. He couldn't handle one more minute of being accused of something he hadn't done. Hadn't he been doing his best to be the outstanding representative of his country his parents wanted him to be?

Anger and frustration had him wanting to punch something, and he knew he needed a calming distraction. And the one thing that always gave him perspective and helped him remember what was really important was spending time with innocent new babies, some of whom were struggling with far more serious problems than he had. Much more important than parental disapproval and gossip and damned fabrications that shouldn't be more than an inconvenient annoyance to be ignored.

Just three steps into NICU he stopped, struck by the picture in front of him. The beautiful profile of Gabriella Cain as she sat next to Skye's incubator, her fire-streaked golden hair tucked behind her ears. Unaware that anyone was looking at her, every emotion was visible. Her eyes and lips, her posture, and the way her fingers gently stroked the infant's tiny arm exposed a mix of emotions so raw his chest tightened to see them. Sadness and anguish.

Guilt. And a longing so naked he knew this was far more than a woman simply looking at the miracle of a newborn.

What had happened to Gabriella to bring this kind of pain to her life?

He watched her for long minutes, uncertain whether to approach her with comfort or quietly leave her alone. His feet seemed to make the decision for him, and he found himself right next to her, his hand reaching to slowly stroke down her soft hair then rest on her slumped shoulder with a gentle squeeze.

She didn't react immediately. It seemed to take her a moment to emerge from whatever dark and private place she was in. Then she turned and looked up at him. Her professional mask slipped across her face, covering all that starkly haunted emotion.

"Have you come to see Skye? She's doing really well." Gabriella stood to give him room to move closer to the incubator, and his hand fell from her shoulder. But he didn't want to see the baby now as much as he wanted to be there for Gabriella. "I left Cameron a short time ago," she said. "She's resting, but asked me to check on Skye and report back. Not that she hasn't gotten reports about every fifteen minutes from various members of the nursing staff. But she isn't quite convinced that's enough."

Her smile seemed forced and it didn't banish the sadness from her eyes. He wanted to reach out to her. He wanted to hold her close and console her for whatever hurt she was holding inside. He wanted to tell her it would be okay, that all pain faded and nothing was forever. And as his eyes met her somber brown ones, he knew.

He wanted to know Gabriella a whole lot better, and to hell with lying low and living like a saint. He couldn't care about gossip or stupid photos or even his mother's embarrassment and worries. Right then, the only thing he cared about was spending time with Gabriella and finding a way to make her smile again.

"My updates from the pediatricians have been good enough that I think we can move Skye into her mama's room," he said. "That would keep Cameron happier and save some time and footsteps by the nursing staff, don't you think?"

"Yes. But of course I don't mind checking on the baby. She's beautiful, isn't she? I'm so happy she's all right."

That wistful look crept across her face again, and Rafael found himself reaching for her hand before he even realized it. "I have a favor to ask of you."

"A favor?"

"Yes. Freya told me that all the recent high-profile operations for Bright Hope patients have the cream of L.A. society lining up to hold exclusive fundraisers, so she's asked if I can attend a charity ball. Since I'm new to Los Angeles and have no one to ask to go with me, would you please come? I'm sure you know all the great things the clinic does for people who don't have easy access to good medical care. Including pregnant women. Wouldn't attending the fundraiser together be a great way for both of us to help continue creating awareness for a good cause?"

The eyes staring at him were wide and stunned. Why, he wasn't sure, since they'd dined together the night before. Surely if she'd heard about the photo and gossip, she would have said so. Still, she just stood there, her lips parted but mute.

"Is my English not as good as I think it is? I asked if you'd attend a party with me. Did I accidentally ask you to eat worms?" he teased, hoping to get a real smile and a yes from her.

"Um, no. Your English, as you well know, is better than most who speak it as a first language." The smile she gave him was strained, but it was a start. "But I'm afraid I can't come with you."

"Why not?"

"It just…wouldn't be right. Excuse me while I check back with Cameron."

He watched her tear from the room as though that gorgeous hair of hers was actually on fire and not just shimmering with flaming hues. He wasn't used to being turned down flat and wondered if it just might have to do with her running from the barely banked-down heat they'd shared last night.

Remembering that the whole reason he'd come to NICU had been to find some inner calm, he turned to little Skye, sweetly and innocently lying in her crib. But he wasn't really seeing her. He was seeing Gabriella's expression as she'd looked at the infant, and he knew without a doubt that whatever had caused that anguish was something she'd been carrying for too long.

Yes, he'd been given orders from headquarters—which meant his parents—to hide from the past, unwelcome limelight for a while. And maybe it would be a mistake to expose Gabriella and whatever secrets she carried to the heavy weight of that microscope along with him. But thinking about her somehow told him with absolute certainty that hiding wasn't the answer. Not for him, and not for Gabriella. It was time for both of them to put their pasts behind them, and the first steps to making that happen would take place at a certain charity ball. A ball with plenty of supporters. Allies who'd be more than happy to convince her to attend with him.

CHAPTER SIX

"EVERYTHING LOOKS GREAT, Freya, with baby the perfect size for a healthy fetus, four months in gestation," Gabby said, smiling. "And you look wonderful too. Your skin is positively glowing. Can I admit to being jealous?"

She'd said the words to make Freya happy, but right after she'd spoken them, the unpleasant, unexpected, and unwelcome cloud weightily slipped over her head again. Why were the memories becoming more frequent, instead of more distant? She had no idea, but dwelling on it accomplished nothing, and she did her best to shake off the gray gloom, because Freya deserved the true joy Gabby felt for her friend and employer.

"I do feel wonderful, honestly." Freya's smile was big enough to banish some of Gabby's moping and make her smile too. "Though several friends have told me to enjoy it while it lasts, because after it arrives I'll be so sleep-deprived I'll forget the baby's name."

Freya's words dashed the final remnants of gloom, and Gabby had to laugh. "Maybe not quite that much. But no matter how many times I warn new mothers that a lot of babies refuse to sleep, no one really hears it until they're living it."

"Well, either way, sleep or no sleep, I'm beyond excited." Freya sat up and adjusted her exam gown. "Half-dressed isn't the way to talk business, but since we're both so busy I'm going to take advantage of this time alone to chat."

"About?"

"The charity ball. Rafael Moreno told me he asked you to go with him, but you told him you didn't want to." Her voice became chiding. "Really, Gabby, why in the world would you say that?"

Her stomach plunged and tightened as she stared at Freya in surprise. How was she supposed to answer that? *Oh, I find him too sexy and attractive, that's all, and my life is devoted to my work now.*

"Well, he's a little overbearing, don't you think? And arrogant."

And unbearably hot.

"I think it's confidence more than arrogance," Freya said with a smile. "But you don't have to be best friends with him, or even particularly like him, to attend the ball with him, Gabby. The purpose of the fundraiser is to raise awareness and money for the Bright Hope Clinic. When one of our own obstetricians, temporary or not, who happens to also be a *prince* attends the ball, that's news. Like it or not, that's the way the world works. Rafael pointed out to me that if the head midwife at the hospital is the prince's date for the night, that's even bigger news, and exactly the kind of public relations opportunity I'm always looking for."

How weird was it that Freya's words sent Gabby's stomach sinking in dread at the same time her chest lifted in excitement and her darned subconscious immediately imagined what kind of dress she should wear to such an event? Clearly Rafael Moreno's arrival at The Hollywood Hills Clinic had sent her sanity a little off-kilter, since she really should be annoyed that he'd gotten Freya involved, using that kind of manipulation to get her to attend with him. Another example of the man's colossal ego!

But even if her entire body had been filled with dread instead of that peculiar mixture of emotions, it wasn't like she could say no. She believed in what the Bright Hope Clinic was doing, and if she could contribute in any way, big or small, she wanted to.

"Fine. I'll go." She hoped Freya didn't notice that her gruffly sighed answer was charged with anticipation too. After all, what woman in her right mind—or even confused one—wouldn't want to be Cinderella for just one night, attending a ball with a handsome prince?

She'd just have to be sure to leave her glass slippers buried deep in her closet at home.

When Gabby had decided to install a new top-to-bottom door mirror in her closet, she'd never dreamed that she'd be needing it to look at herself in a long gown. A gown she'd be wearing to attend a ball with a handsome prince. Gabby snorted and shook her head at herself, wondering how a grown woman could feel so wrapped up in thinking about a party and what she'd be wearing, like a teenager going to the prom. Ridiculous.

She studied the lines of her dress. Turned side to side, looked at the back, then the front again. And sighed. Because she knew full well that the majority of women attending the ball tonight would be wearing designer dresses that cost more than her month's rent, not to mention that there wouldn't be a single one there who'd made her own gown.

Filled with jitters of doubt now, she worried that maybe she shouldn't have done that. Why had she been so convinced she shouldn't just buy one off the rack? The answer was because she knew anything she could afford would be made from substandard fabrics, compared to the glamorous, designer dresses the rich and famous would be wearing tonight. And she knew how to sew, didn't she?

Her strong, female ancestors had not only studied midwifery and spent their lives helping others, they'd been talented seamstresses. Hadn't learning at her grandmother and mother's knees given her the skills to pull this off? Staring at her dress now, she wasn't so sure. The ring of her doorbell…a loud, silly horse whinny the previous avid horseracing fan tenants had installed…made her jump. Then laugh out loud. Clearly Cinderella's carriage had arrived, except the prince was already on board, not waiting at the ball.

Resisting the urge to wipe her suddenly sweaty hands down the emerald-green fabric of her gown, she opened the front door. Then stared, her breath hitching.

She'd thought Dr. Rafael Moreno had been attractive in the scrubs that showed his strong physique? In a dress shirt and pants at the clinic, and when they'd gone to dinner? Those Rafael Morenos had nothing on this one, who exuded royal arrogance from head to toe in a tuxedo that fitted him so perfectly she knew it had to have been tailor-made for him. His shirt was so white it was practically blinding, his classic black bow tie perfectly placed beneath his strong, tanned throat. The late evening sun gleamed on his dark, glossy hair and sculpted jawline, and a slow smile curved his lips.

She gulped. There was one perfect way to describe how her body was reacting to his mouthwatering beauty.

Tuxedo libido.

She fought down a nervous giggle. How had the room gotten so warm? Clearly, May in Los Angeles meant it was time to adjust the thermostat.

"Hi," she said, knowing she sounded a little breathless,

but since she *was* breathless it was the best she could do. "I'm ready. I just need to grab my purse."

"I'm relieved, I have to say."

"That I'm ready? Is that another comment about what you think of my organizational skills?"

"No. As I drove here, I wasn't sure what to expect, having several scenarios that came to mind. In the first, I was afraid you'd open the door wearing sweatpants, planning to ditch me to lounge at home instead, since you hadn't wanted to come with me tonight."

"I wouldn't ditch you, even though you'd have deserved it if I did, since it was pretty sneaky of you to get Freya involved as your date planner. However, I always honor my commitments. Though I admit that lounging in sweatpants holds a certain appeal."

"To me as well. You would look very sexy in sweatpants."

"Uh-huh. Pretty sure sexy and sweatpants are mutually exclusive."

"Not true. I'm picturing you in them right now." Something about the way he was looking at her had her wondering exactly what he was picturing, and her breath hitched all over again. "The other, even worse scenario I envisioned was you wearing a more casual dress because you were planning to go on a date with someone else. In which case, I'd have to fight him when he came to pick you up, and my parents rarely appreciate that kind of scene."

Despite the absurd words, there was something serious in the gleam of his eyes that had her laughing in surprise. "I can't see you fighting over a woman. There are too many fish in the sea who'd fall at your feet for a date, because they don't know what a shark you are."

"But you're willing to risk a date with a shark for a good cause, hmm? And there's only one woman as beautiful and interesting as you are. That dress is exquisite on you, by the way. My mother would be impressed with your designer."

She laughed. and at the same time a bubble of satisfaction and relief that she didn't look ridiculous filled her chest. "Don't tell anyone, but the designer is someone who works for a dress-pattern company, and I made it myself."

"You made it yourself?" The astonishment on his face was comical. "That's incredible! Beautiful, compassionate, and talented as well. Every man at the ball tonight will envy my good fortune to have you on my arm."

It was a line, she knew, but her stomach flipped inside out anyway. "They'll probably envy you for a lot of other reasons, like that whole prince thing that makes you think you can do whatever you want whenever you want." Okay, she didn't really think he was an overbearing jerk anymore, but it was probably a good idea to keep up that charade.

She also wouldn't add all the other reasons men would envy him. Like his incredible good looks and confidence and sense of humor and everything else about him that made every part of her body tingle a little. She turned jerkily to grab her evening bag from the chair, willing herself to act normal and calm. After all, this wasn't a real date. The only reason he'd asked—no, manipulated—her to join him tonight was because it was good PR for the clinic, and more publicity about the ball would result in more donations.

His grasp on her elbow was light, but Gabby still felt the warmth of it clear to her toes as he tucked her into the car. Her heart seemed to thunder as much as the car engine as it accelerated around the mountain curves. Excitement pumped through her veins, and she realized she hadn't felt this…this *alive* in a very long time. Not since her life, which she'd thought had been so steady and planned out, had been obliterated with one, selfishly bad decision.

She determinedly squelched those thoughts. No point in dwelling on something she couldn't change when she had a few hours to enjoy what she knew would be a very special evening. She stole a look at the man sitting so very close to her and he must have felt her gaze because he glanced at her with a smile that suddenly faded.

"There's one thing I must warn you about," he said, turning his attention back to the road. "I'm frequently followed by the press, looking for a juicy story. I would guess there will be photographers outside the hotel anyway, wanting to get pictures of the various stars attending this event. Some will doubtless take pictures of us too, so don't let it worry you."

"Do you often give them juicy stories?"

"If you asked my parents, they'd say yes. In fact, I'll tell you the truth. I came to stay in L.A. for two reasons. To see James and to hide from the press after an unfortunate incident."

"I can't imagine you hiding from anyone."

"I don't like to. But there are times that even I have to bow to family pressures, and this was one of them. But I've decided I don't care. That being out with you tonight is important to me—and I hope you won't let any media coverage bother you either."

"The media won't care who I am, so I'm not worried about it."

"Don't count on that."

His expression looked almost grim as he pulled the car up to the front doors of the hotel. Gabby stared in shock at the swarm of people wielding cameras and standing on both sides of the huge double doors, kept back by red velvet ropes curving between golden stanchions. A valet opened her door and in mere seconds Rafael appeared by her side, reaching for her hand. The camera flashes were so bright and constant it was like being hit in the face with a strobe light, and she blinked and instinctively reeled back. Rafael's hand dropped hers to move to the small of her back, firm and steady. He seemed unfazed by it all, leading her forward in an even, unhurried pace until they were safely inside the hotel doors held open by employees.

"Oh, my Lord, you weren't kidding!" She stared at him. "Is it like this wherever you go?"

"Not always. When there's an event they know I'll be showing up for, yes. But sometimes, as you saw when we had dinner the other night, they're not around. Or it can seem that way, though sometimes I'm wrong about that."

As they moved farther into the room, she quickly looked around, expecting cameras to be closing in on them at that very moment. Thankfully, all she saw was a room filled with beautifully dressed men and women, all smiling and talking against the gorgeous backdrop of an old-style hotel, built in the days when Hollywood had been all glitter and gold and extravagance.

"Gabriella, there is something I need to talk to you about regarding the paparazzi," Rafael said.

She turned to him, wondering what was causing that crease between his brows, but whatever he'd been about to say was interrupted by the arrival of several people eager to talk to him. Then others. More as they wandered through the crowds, taking bites of amazing hors d'oeuvres and sips of champagne, and it was obvious that more than one woman admired her date for the night, and were looking at *her* with envy, not the other way around, as Rafael had flatteringly predicted.

"Rafael, Gabby, I see my sister nudged you into coming tonight," James Rothsberg said as he appeared next to them. Held in the curve of his arm was the stunning woman Gabby had recently seen photographed with him in a few tabloid spreads.

"Does Freya ever nudge anyone into anything?" Rafael said with a grin. "Strong-armed is more like it, but I'm glad to be here for such a great cause, and I know Gabriella cares a lot about underprivileged children too."

"I'm so happy to be helping spread the word about the Bright Hope Clinic," Gabby said. "Not to mention getting to eat all the wonderful food here tonight." She stopped there, even though she would have liked to note that Rafael was pretty good at strong-arm tactics himself.

"Freya's a force of nature, for sure. I'm glad you were able to make it." James grinned and introduced them to his date, who seemed to study Rafael with extreme interest before glancing at Gabby.

"Such a pretty dress," she said with what looked like an oddly amused smile, and Gabby froze, wondering if it was obvious she'd made it herself. "Did you choose the color of it to go with your date's eyes? Quite a striking color."

Well, that was even worse than noticing it was homemade. Embarrassment streaked through Gabby's whole body, ending with her cheeks scorching as she realized her dress really was almost exactly the same color as Rafael's eyes. Would anyone else think she'd done it on purpose, like they were attending a high school homecoming dance together or something? Or, worse, had she chosen the fabric unconsciously thinking of his mesmerizing gaze?

"My goodness, you're right! I hadn't even noticed that," she managed to say, struggling to make her tone sound light and amused too. "My mother drummed into me that people with strawberry blonde hair like hers and mine should wear green whenever possible and avoid red so as not to look like a spark plug."

"She looks amazing in green, doesn't she?" Rafael

said smoothly, before turning to Gabby. "Though there's no possibility that tall, slender you could ever resemble a spark plug."

The seeming sincerity joining the gleam in his eyes made her blush all over again. "Thank you."

"You probably know how lucky The Hollywood Hills Clinic is to have her running the maternity ward, James. She's not only a skilled midwife, she has a way with patients that makes every one of them more than glad they're there. Thanks for giving me the opportunity to work with her."

"Gabby's the best. And you'd better not think of stealing her away to some hospital in the Mediterranean when you leave, Rafael, or I'll have to tell secrets about you that you wouldn't want shared."

Obviously just kidding, James's eyes twinkled as he spoke, but Rafael seemed a little more serious when he looked down at Gabby. "We all have secrets, don't we? Sometimes sharing them is a good thing, don't you think?"

Heart skittering, she didn't answer, wondering what he meant. Could he somehow know about her past and her mistakes?

No. Impossible. Freya knew she'd had a bad breakup before coming to work at the clinic, but not the reason for it, and that was the way Gabby wanted to keep it.

"Sometimes. But usually it's best to keep our secrets to ourselves." James's smile had flatlined too, as he and his date said their goodbyes and went to mingle with the crowd.

"Let's dance, shall we?"

Oh, goodness. Dance? Close to him? "I don't think—"

But in typical Rafael fashion he didn't wait for her to finish her answer before setting his glass on the tray of a passing waiter then wrapping his hand around hers to move to the dance floor. When he turned to face her, his other palm slid from her waist to the small of her back. She slipped her hand up the soft fabric of his jacket to rest it on his shoulder, and her breath caught in her throat as she looked up at him.

The orchestra struck up a new tune, and they began to move. "Thank you for coming with me tonight."

"Thank you for inviting me. It's been lovely."

"Even though you didn't want to at first?"

"Even though." She wasn't about to tell him why, and at the moment that seemed unfathomable. Because being so close to him, with all that heat from his body skimming across her bare arms and décolletage, felt wonderful.

On a slow turn, he brought her close enough that her breasts brushed his chest, and he lowered his mouth closer to her ear. "So why didn't you want to, Gabriella?"

"Because you're arrogant and bossy."

"Yes. Among other things." The chandelier cast light and shadows across his chiseled face and the bow of his lips as he smiled. "I thought we worked out a few of those issues when we went to dinner together. Which reminds me, I have to tell you something."

"What?"

His smile had disappeared and when he opened his mouth to answer he hesitated. Then, to her surprise, the words that came out were, "Uh-oh," and his attention seemed to be grabbed by something behind her.

She turned to see James standing mostly hidden at the back of the room behind the band. With him, instead of his date, was Mila Brightman and even from this distance it was obvious that Mila was hopping mad about something, and giving it to James with both barrels.

"Oh, dear. What do you think is wrong?"

"I don't know. I hope it's not— Never mind." A deep

frown creased Rafael's brow as he shook his head. "I was about to tell you—"

But before he could finish, the band stopped playing and Freya stepped onto the platform to speak into the microphone about the event and why they were all there tonight. After thanking the hosts and giving some details about the Bright Hope Clinic, she advised everyone to enjoy desserts and drinks as there would shortly be a video presentation about some of the patients who'd been helped there.

"I don't know about you, but I think we've done our duty," Rafael said, leaning close to speak in her ear. "What do you say to a little dine and dash?"

"Dine and dash? Do princes do that? I have to admit the mental image of you gobbling food then furtively sneaking out the door is hard to picture." Since she hadn't seen him any way but tall, proud, and very visible, that was an understatement. "But I can't say I'd complain about leaving soon. I'm about talked out."

"You know how it is, trying to say goodbyes and exit an event like this. Takes at least another hour, so let's get the process started."

She didn't, really. If she walked out the door that second, she was quite sure not a soul would bother her, but she'd already seen the attention Rafael garnered, and could well believe he'd be stopped by half the crowd en route.

Which was exactly what happened. And each time he was stopped he took pains to draw her into the conversation. Not only did he introduce her to everyone with glowing compliments about her skills as a midwife, stating again how lucky The Hollywood Hills Clinic was to have her, there was something else in his eyes and expression as he did so.

Something that didn't seem like simple professional admiration. Instead, it felt much more personal.

That odd mix of excitement and dismay rolled around her belly all over again, which was dangerous. Yes, it was a magical night. But she couldn't let the magic of it allow her to forget. She couldn't risk a relationship with any man, even one as amazing as Rafael. And, yes, she knew a man like Rafael Moreno would want only a fling, but even that would be too much.

Why was she even thinking he'd want that, anyway? Must be the Cinderella feeling she'd had all evening, wearing a dress far fancier than she'd ever worn before, on a date with pretty much the world's most handsome bachelor prince. The feel of his big, possessive hand holding hers or resting on her lower back. The compliments. The way he looked at her for long moments as though they were totally alone.

She shook her head fiercely at herself. The man doubtless acted like that with all women at parties, and especially those on a date with him, and to read anything more into it was plain foolish. Probably flirting came to him as naturally as the charm he'd exuded all evening. As naturally as the arrogant rudeness he'd bestowed on her when they'd first met.

Any woman would be intrigued by a multifaceted man like Rafael Moreno. None of it meant a thing—not his flirting and not the googly eyes she caught herself making at him. Tomorrow she'd be wearing her scrubs again, they'd go back to their normal, cordial working relationship and tonight would be forgotten.

Trying to bring her mind back to the conversation, she watched his mouth move as he talked to friends of James he obviously knew, and the sensuality of his lips pretty much obliterated all her previous self-scolding. Her ability to converse. Her thoughts instead drifted to all wrong ones that gave her tummy a different kind of funny feeling. A feeling that she'd give her next paycheck to kiss him once, just to see how it would feel. Just once. Once before the strike of midnight—was that so much to ask?

She stared in fascination as he took a sip of his drink and his tongue licked a tiny drop from his lip. And with breathless certainty she knew. The man would be one amazing kisser.

"You probably agree with that, don't you, Gabriella?"

Rafael had turned fully to her, the slight curve of his lips fading as their eyes met, and she foggily realized the people he'd been talking to had moved on. Several beats passed as they just stared at one another, and Gabby wished she had some idea how to answer him but had no clue.

His lids lowered slightly, and something hot and alive flickered inside that deep green. "You weren't listening at all, were you, *bella*?" He stepped closer, his voice a low rumble. "Something else on your mind?"

Yeah. Oh, yeah, but I'm not saying what. Except she had a bad feeling it was written in red neon on her forehead for him to see anyway. Frantically trying to come up with an answer that wasn't incriminating, she managed one word. "Sweatpants."

A slow smile creased his face and made his eyes gleam. "Mine too, Gabriella. Let's get out of here."

"I don't believe you even own sweatpants."

"Not true. I have all the latest designers' versions in every color, like any prince should."

"Now you're making fun of me. I wasn't saying you wouldn't have any because you're a prince, it's because...because...oh, never mind." He might have been saying sweet and complimentary things about her all night, but it still felt strange to tell him what she'd been thinking. Which was that he exuded a regal confidence all too well suited by the tuxedo he wore. Then again, that same presence filled any room he was in at the clinic, even wearing scrubs, so clearly it had nothing to do with what he wore.

Or what he didn't.

Shocked at the sudden fantasy of what he might look like naked, which she sort of, kind of almost knew, she pinched her lips closed so she wouldn't say anything completely embarrassing as he opened the car door. So focused on her thoughts and, well, truthfully, on *him* and his sheer, breathtaking masculinity as he held her hand, she barely noticed the dozens of flashbulbs lighting the night. His big body shielded her from the cameras as he tucked her into his car before sliding into the driver's seat.

"Seat belt on?" The engine roared to life as he turned the key in the ignition, pausing to look at her with one eyebrow quirked.

"Yes."

"Good." The car rolled slowly forward for about ten feet, then took off like a rocket down the curve and onto the main road.

CHAPTER SEVEN

THE GROWLING SPORTS car's sudden acceleration shoved Gabby back into the sumptuously curved leather seat, and she gasped then chuckled. "You must be in a hurry to get into those sweatpants."

He didn't answer. Just looked at her with that glint in his eyes. A gaze so unnerving she felt like he might be seeing something clear down in her soul she didn't want him to see. He was close, so close to her inside the small confines of the car it seemed he'd sucked every bit of oxygen completely out of the space, making it very hard to breathe.

"Um, you're making me nervous," she finally said. "If you're looking at me, that means you're not looking at the road, and if I have to die, I want equal billing in the headlines."

"Equal billing?" His gaze finally moved to the road, and she let out a relieved breath. "What do you mean?"

"You know, instead of 'Prince Rafael Moreno and some other person die in car crash,' I'd like to at least get 'Joe Schmoe and Gabby Cain plunge into a canyon to their deaths.'"

He laughed. "And here I would have thought you didn't crave publicity, like most of our patients do."

"I'm kidding, of course. Believe me, the last thing I would ever want is my name splashed in the papers for any reason." Not that it would ever happen to her. But she'd seen enough times when patients got publicity they'd originally wanted, only to have it result in reporters digging deep into details of their lives they didn't want shared.

"I've been in the media since the day I was born. You get used to it."

"I didn't get what that might be like, not really, until all those cameras flashed in my face. It may be just a part of life for people like you and Cameron Fontaine, but I bet it's still not fun." And suddenly it struck her that someone just might want to put a name to *her* face. Some unknown woman attending tonight's party with a Mediterranean prince. Her stomach tightened at the thought, until she remembered that Freya had made a big, public deal out of her being a midwife at The Hollywood Hills Clinic. Surely that's all they would report. Probably no one would feel a need to look beyond that.

The car ground to a halt against the curb in front of her apartment. Rafael turned off the engine and the sudden quiet seemed to ring in her ears along with her rapid heartbeat. He had that look in his eyes again. The one he'd had all evening, as though he thought she was special. Beautiful, which he'd said, but men so often didn't mean what they said, she knew. Sometimes their words were a thoughtless, casual compliment, or a tactic to get sex, or a way to distract a woman from starting important conversations.

And yet when Rafael complimented her, it didn't feel like any of those things. It struck her that, other than the appreciation she often got from her patients, she hadn't felt special to anyone in a very long time.

The last time she had, it had proven to be a mirage. Evaporating when she'd messed up so badly. Her mistake had broken her heart. Then, along with being heartbroken, she'd been suddenly alone, just when she'd needed support and love more than at any other time in her life.

She drew in a breath, shoved the pain of those negative memories aside, and stomped on them for good measure. Wasn't she Cinderella, just for tonight? Maybe she didn't really deserve happiness, but this evening Rafael had made her feel wonderful and carefree, and she wasn't quite ready for the evening, and those good feelings, to end.

"Would you…like to come in for coffee?"

The eyes that seemed to be studying her with questions in them warmed, crinkling at the corners as he smiled. "I'd like that very much."

Once inside, she ushered him to sit down, and her belly quivered with a maelstrom of nerves and excitement. She'd lived in L.A. for two years but had never had even one man in her apartment. There'd been good reason for that, and there still was, but tonight was a fairy tale, right? One evening before her life went back to normal at midnight.

"Feel free to change into those sweats so you're more comfortable," he said, slipping off his tuxedo jacket and settling himself onto one side of her sofa. "I would if I could."

She watched his long, tanned fingers pull the end of his bow tie, sliding it off before slowly unbuttoning his top shirt buttons, revealing a bronzed throat. Then realized she was just standing there motionless, practically mooning over the man.

Yep. Tuxedo libido all right.

"I think I'll do that. Be right back."

Alone in her room, she felt a twinge of regret at having to take off the dress that had made her feel like she was floating as they'd danced around the ballroom. But it would feel silly, not to mention uncomfortable, to be sitting in her living room in a long gown. As she slid off her clothes, the brief thought of Rafael walking into her room and sweeping her into his arms shortened her breath, but at the same time she laughed at herself. Definitely too much fairy-tale fantasy going on in her head tonight! One thing she was sure of—arrogant or not, playboy reputation or not, he wasn't the kind of man to do something inappropriate like that.

She quickly slipped into a T-shirt and the shapeless, comfy sweatpants they'd joked about, feeling even more unisex in them than the scrubs she wore most days. But if she put on jeans to look at least marginally attractive, he might know why. As the thoughts pinged around in her brain she rolled her eyes at herself and snorted. "Get a grip on yourself, Gabby. He's probably just here to be polite."

But when she emerged to walk across the living room, the way his gaze tracked her made her feel like she still had that gown on after all. Heart thudding, she made coffee in her small kitchen that opened to the living room so she could still see him, watching her in a way that was unnerving but exciting.

"Do you take cream or sugar?"

"Just black."

She handed him the cup, hyperaware of the feel of his fingers sliding against hers as he took it. Then stood there hesitating, probably looking like a fool, as she pondered whether or not to sit next to him on the sofa or several, discreet feet away in a chair.

The decision was made for her when he reached for her hand and gave it a gentle tug. "Sit by me. You can curl up in comfort a lot better here than over there."

"How did you know this is my curling-up corner? Was I eyeing it longingly?"

"You could say that."

Oh, Lord. Maybe he'd spotted her eyeing *him* longingly. Breaking eye contact with that amused green, she took longer than necessary to slide her cup onto a coaster before scrunching up in the corner as far away from him as possible. Which was still just a couple feet from him. She needed a distraction, and picked her cup up to take a sip, eyeing him over the rim, wondering if the heat radiating through her body was from his nearness or the coffee. She had a bad feeling it had nothing to do with her drink.

Despite loosening his top shirt buttons, there was no way he could be described as being able to "curl up in comfort."

"I feel bad you're still in your starched finery, but I don't think anything I have here would fit you."

"Which is a good thing, as I always feel a little strange when I'm at a woman's home and she opens a wardrobe of men's clothes for me to choose from."

"Does that really happen?"

"More than you'd guess. Which is one of the many reasons spending time with you is like breathing in fresh air."

"Does that line usually work for you?"

"It's one I haven't used before, because I meant it." His eyes gleamed. "Maybe you can tell me how well it works."

She gulped. Should she tell him that just hearing that deep, sexy voice of his recite the alphabet might make her jump into his lap? If she'd been a different kind of woman, that was. A woman interested in being with a man. "I'm not much of an expert on lines men use, so I'm not a good person to ask."

"If that's true, the men in Los Angeles must not be very bright. You're not only beautiful, in the short time I've known you I've seen you're smart and caring and feisty and damned special. And I promise that's not a line."

The amusement had left his face, and his expression was utterly serious as he looked at her. Gabby felt her heart melting and thudding and had no idea what she was supposed to say in response. Maybe compliment him too?

"And I've seen that you're not the arrogant jerk I thought you were. Just a doctor who does what it takes to make things right for a patient, whether it's good medical care, empathy, or humor. Princely attitude notwithstanding."

"Thank you. I think." He smiled again. "Is that what's called a backhanded compliment? But I probably deserve both the good and bad from it. So tell me. Why do you work so much? So many double shifts? And when you're not working, why do you keep mostly to yourself?"

Startled by the turn of the conversation, she found herself hesitating, for a split second feeling a shocking need to share her past, her mistakes. Her pain. But that was ridiculous. She didn't talk to anyone about it. She barely knew Rafael, and he probably wouldn't want their evening together to be spoiled by a depressing conversation. Not to mention that the last thing she needed was for everyone at the hospital to know who she really was. "I love my job. And who says I keep mostly to myself?"

"Freya. James. Even if they hadn't, I've seen it just in the short time I've been here. Seen a sadness that you carry with you." He reached to grasp her hand again, his touch warm and comforting and somehow arousing all at the same time. "What makes you sad, Gabriella?"

"I... Nothing." Just the bittersweet part of her job, bringing babies into the world to loving parents who wanted them. Praying they never had to know how it felt to lose one. "How about you? What makes Rafael Moreno travel the world, working hard and playing hard?"

"Different reasons. But one I just found out? Once in a very long while I'm lucky to meet someone remarkable I enjoy being with." He moved closer, his fingers slipping beneath her chin to bring her gaze to the darkening green one staring at her. “Someone who makes me feel strangely happy in a way I didn't even realize I wanted to.”

She stared in breathless fascination as his mouth slowly lowered to hers, giving her time to protest or pull away, but she found she wanted his kiss. Wanted it with a desperation new to her experience. Had wanted it, if she was honest, all the hours they'd spent together.

His lips touched hers, warm and soft and gentle. Not demanding or insistent or aggressive, as she would have expected a man like him to kiss. No, it was the sweetest kiss she'd ever experienced in her life, his mouth moving slowly and surely on hers, giving and taking, and the longer it went on the more her heart liquefied into a puddle of want for him.

The fingers beneath her chin slipped across her jaw, his wide palm cupping her cheek as the kiss deepened, heated, and Gabby was glad she was half lying down or she was sure she'd have fallen down.

“Gabriella.” His usually almost nonexistent accent thickened slightly as he spoke against her mouth. “I knew you would taste *delicioso*.”

“It's...the coffee.”

She could feel him smile even as he kept pressing soft kisses to her lips. “No, *belleza*, it's most definitely you.”

A sigh of pleasure left her lips as the kiss went from slow and sweet to hot and wet and so earth-shattering she found herself clutching his muscled shoulders and hanging on for dear life. His palms had moved from her face to tangle in her hair, turning her head to the perfect angle for a deep, mind-blowing kiss. Dazed, she realized one hand had moved down to slip beneath her T-shirt, tracking across her skin in a slow caress that made her shiver, finally resting on her breast through her bra.

"I...see now why you wanted me to change out of my dress."

"I was just thinking of your comfort. And I still am." He surprised her by moving his hand off her breast to caress her ribs again, pressing another soft kiss to her mouth, and she quivered at the tenderness of it. "Obviously, I want you. But not if the Gabriella who mostly keeps to herself will regret it tomorrow. You know I'm here for only a little while, and I have a feeling you're not a woman comfortable with making love with a man who's not able to stick around long."

"Not normally, I admit." But she'd learned not to expect someone to stick around, hadn't she? And as she looked into the green of his eyes, dark and questioning and filled with the same intoxicating desire she was feeling, she knew with certainty that tonight was the one time to change that. "I'm content with my life as it is. But I want you, too. And tonight I feel like being Cinderella, making love with you before I turn back into plain old Gabby Cain at midnight."

"That's the worst description of you imaginable." He seemed to study her a long moment, and she wasn't sure what he was seeing, or looking for. His fingertips traced her cheekbone as his thumb caressed her bottom lip. "You, Gabriella Cain, take my breath away."

Then he kissed her again, slowly and deeply, taking her breath away, too. The kiss held so much promise of delicious, incredible sex she uttered a sound of protest when he stopped. "Are you absolutely sure? Because I need to know now or it might kill me to stop."

"I'm sure, okay?" He appeared so suddenly hesitant she was afraid he'd leap up and leave, which might kill *her*. "Take my word for it. The last thing I want is to end up in a Mediterranean prison for killing a prince."

He chuckled against her mouth. "The prisons at home

don't have as many rats as they used to, but it's probably still wise to stay out of them."

"That's my plan."

"Good. Coincides well with mine." She gasped as his lips moved to her jaw, down to her throat, touching the sensitive spot beneath her ear as he deftly flicked the front clasp of her bra open. "I'm wondering if you're perhaps overly warm. I know I am."

Before she could even form an answer, he'd somehow managed to slip her T-shirt over her head and her bra straps down her arms and was staring at her nakedness. His eyes were dark and slashes of color rode high on his cheekbones as his gaze scorched her. Her heart thumped so hard against her ribs she thought he might actually be able to see it pounding.

"You are even more beautiful than I envisioned, *mi ángel*." The glide of his touch across her breasts felt nearly reverent as his gaze returned to hers, and even as she was shocked that she was doing this, letting herself be with a man again, with *this* man in particular, she wanted him more than she could ever remember wanting anyone.

He kissed her again, hotter and more intense, lying nearly on top of her now, pressing her into the cushions, and the small groan that left his mouth and swirled into hers just about set her on fire. Knowing he was as aroused as she was had her arching her back for more, pressing her breasts against him, only to discover it wasn't enough to feel his shirt there. She wanted his skin against hers, and fumbled to get the shirt open and off.

Except she hadn't done this for a long time, and never with a tuxedo shirt, which she was learning had aggravatingly difficult buttons, and couldn't manage to make it happen. Her sounds of frustration made him smile against her mouth before he leaned back.

"Let me, *bella*."

In a slow striptease, he worked the buttons one by one, his lips curved at the same time his eyes smoldered, intently focused on her as she watched him. Inch by torturous inch, he exposed a chest even more muscled than she remembered, his bronzed skin covered with dark hair that looked as soft and silky and outrageously manly as the rest of him.

Mouth dry, she knew with certainty that this was truly a Cinderella night. That she'd never again be with a man as physically perfect as Prince Rafael Moreno, and she still couldn't quite wrap her brain around the fact that he wanted to be with her as much as she wanted to be with him.

Then she couldn't admire his chest anymore because he lowered himself to her, his bare and scorchingly hot torso pressed against hers. He kissed her again, and she practically drowned in the deliciousness of it all. Her bones turned to utter liquid when he skimmed that talented mouth down her throat, across her collarbone, then on to her breasts. Gasping, her hands burrowed into the thick softness of his hair as he ministered to one nipple, then the other, and she didn't care that she was making little sounds and moving beneath him and pressing against him because control had gone out the window and all she wanted was to experience the incredible way he was making her feel.

Vaguely, she was aware of wide, warm palms slipping inside her sweatpants to cup her rear, then more aware of his hot mouth tracking from her breast down her belly as the pants and panties disappeared off over her feet, leaving her naked. Strong hands slid back up her legs to caress her thighs, his mouth following.

"Rafael." She didn't know what she was going to say,

exactly, and wasn't sure she could talk at all—her breath was so choppy she feared she might hyperventilate.

"Gabriella." His teeth nipped her knee, followed by a teasing lick, moving up to her hipbone, and she jumped with a laughing gasp. "Shall we take this to the bedroom?"

"No. I might combust before then."

A low, masculine laugh full of satisfaction swept across her skin. "*Bueno.* Me as well."

Licking across her quivering belly, he touched her right where she wanted to be touched, and she gasped and wriggled against his talented fingers, until finally she couldn't wait any longer. She reached for him, only to realize his darned pants were still on and completely in the way, just like his shirt had been. "What are your pants doing on? Get them off, fast."

He gave a short laugh. "And you call me bossy?"

"I'm assertive when I need to be. And, believe me, right now I need to be."

His eyes blazed at her with both amusement and heat. "My pants are on because I keep a condom in them. But not for long."

"I appreciate a prepared prince," she managed to say.

Another husky chuckle left his lips as he shucked his pants and took care of the condom, thankfully seeming to be in as much of a hurry as she was. He lowered his body to hers, and she gasped at the amazing sensation as he gently, slowly joined with her body, arching helplessly as they began to move together.

"Cariña. Mi ángel." His whispered words had her blinking open her eyes, and his were the greenest she'd seen them, focused and gleaming and locked on hers. More Spanish words left his lips, first in whispers then louder as they rocked together until she cried out, and he joined with her in a long, low groan that reverberated in her chest.

The way he gathered her against him, tangling his fingers in her hair to tuck her face against his warm throat, felt tender and protective, and Gabby let herself absorb the intimacy and wonder of it. She tried hard not to think about how good it felt, how right, and how, when midnight came, Cinderella would be back in her corner all alone once again.

CHAPTER EIGHT

RAFAEL LISTENED TO the sound of his footsteps echoing across the marble-tiled foyer and wished he'd worn his scrubs and crepe-soled shoes instead, planning to change out of his regular shirt and dress pants if he'd needed to deliver a baby. Then cursed lightly under his breath at himself as he caught himself glancing around guiltily.

When was the last time he'd felt like a boy trying to sneak around undetected? Not since he'd been in primary school, since even before high school most people in authority hadn't felt comfortable disciplining the second-born prince of their country. It was no wonder he'd run a little wild at times.

His various sports adventures, dating adventures, and foolish errors in judgment had been so well documented by the press over the years, he'd believed he was immune to caring about it. And he was immune, really, except that he had to care for Gabriella's sake.

Yes, there were the occasional non-sensationalized stories. Ones that talked about medical school, and the years of study he put in to become a doctor and his actual work. But articles like that didn't seem to hold as much interest for most people as the simple fact that he'd been born under the blessing and curse of royalty.

Not that it was only the public who felt that way, since

his own family was pretty uninterested in his accomplishments. There were those times when he was happy about the press coverage, if it brought attention to the needs of the many women around the world who were underserved by proper medical care—or didn't have access to care at all. But those kinds of stories were unfortunately few and far between.

As he skulked through the clinic, he felt ridiculous. And selfish. Spending time with Gabriella while he was in L.A. was more than good for him, but for her? Not so much. Being out in public with him definitely exposed her to potential embarrassment, with the media sniffing around. To having things publicly spread about her, and whether they were truth or lies wouldn't matter.

He'd dated plenty of women who liked having their faces in the tabloids, holding on to his arm. But Gabriella wasn't like other women. In so many ways. Something about her had grabbed his insides and tugged hard at his soul from the first second he'd met her. Her fiery temper had matched that beautiful hair of hers, then the next second she'd been endearingly sweet and caring with their very difficult patient. Add to that a sexiness she seemed barely aware of and a sadness in the depths of those brown eyes, and she was fascinating with a capital F.

The vision of the smile in her eyes and on her lips as they'd danced last night, the sight of her beautiful naked body as they'd made love, the memories of how her skin had felt against his, had him closing his eyes to hold it all inside. Had him wanting to find her right then, pull her into an empty room, and kiss her breathless.

But she deserved better than him. Deserved more than a man who would only be around for a month or two. Deserved the kind of man who was capable of offering her a commitment and a future, if that was what she wanted. And he wasn't that man.

No. For her sake, he should steer clear of her from now on. Let last night be one great memory for both of them. The last thing he would ever want would be to add to the sadness in her eyes after he'd moved on.

He sighed and, feeling a little bruised, rubbed his chest. Knew that the bruising was inside, not out, but it would heal. At least, he assumed it would. He'd never felt quite like this before, so he couldn't be sure. But it would be far worse to keep seeing Gabriella and bruise her, too.

Time to stop moping and get to work. He stopped at the computer outside one of the nurses' stations to check some charts, and decided to see Cameron Fontaine first. Medically, she was absolutely fine. But she'd wanted to stay at the hospital a little longer, both so she could be near baby Skye and because she didn't want to be seen in public while she was losing her "baby fat."

Rafael and everyone else had reassured her it was hardly noticeable, though he knew many of the new mothers giving birth at the clinic worried about the same thing, having to live in the very close scrutiny of the public eye. Cameron was happy to be eating healthy spa food specially prepared to have the nutrition she needed, while helping her lose weight as she worked with personal fitness trainers. And, Lord knew, a happy Cameron made the lives of everyone in the clinic easier.

Including Gabriella's, and he again marveled at her amazing patience and even empathy with a woman who could be pretty demanding. Then realized his every thought seemed to lead right back to Gabriella. How had his head become so consumed with her in such a short period of time?

Deep in thought on his way to Cameron's room, the

woman on his mind seemed to practically materialize out of thin air. She'd probably come out of the door he'd been about to walk by, but since her face had been what he'd been seeing and not the hallway, it gave him a start to see her actually there.

From the expression on her face, he'd startled her, too. Her face seemed to flush as she stared at him, and she swept her hair behind her ears in a nervous gesture he'd only seen that night in his house when she'd run into his naked chest. The night he'd wanted to kiss her to see how she'd react.

Which reminded him all over again what it had been like to kiss her the night before. Along with all the other things they'd done together over the course of the night, and he had a feeling his face was flushed, too, but not with nervousness. With a heat he'd had a hard time banking down every time he'd thought of her since leaving her in the wee hours of the morning.

"Good morning, Ms. Cain."

"Um, good morning, Dr. Moreno."

Her voice was husky, and her tongue flicked out to lick her lips, and he was damned if all his resolutions to the contrary moments ago didn't fly straight out of his brain. Replaced by that desire to grab her up, take her to the nearest empty room, and kiss her until neither of them could breathe.

"I was about to see Cameron Fontaine," he said, forcing his mind away from the thoughts that were actually making his body hard as they stood there in public. "Have you checked on her this morning?"

"Yes. She's in the gym with the fitness trainer right now, so you'll have to see someone else first. Speaking of which, I have a patient waiting in my office. She's feeling nervous about some pain and wants to talk to me about it. Excuse me."

She turned without another word and hurried down the corridor. He watched her slim rear in her scrubs swaying slightly, which immediately took his thoughts back yet again to last night and how she'd looked in her sweats. Then out of them. Which he'd sworn to himself he'd stop thinking about.

Maybe he needed to hit the clinic gym himself for a long workout, then a nice cold shower.

"Dr. Moreno! Rafael!"

Gabriella's urgent voice had him turning to see her running back in his direction. "What's wrong?"

"We have a precipitous delivery. My patient thought she might be imagining things, but she's already eight centimeters dilated. Would you go and see to her while I get the pre-cep pack? My office."

Rafael strode to the room. Knowing Gabriella knew what she was doing should have prepared him, but he was still surprised to see a woman lying on the floor of Gabriella's office, practically wedged between the chairs in front of her desk, writhing and moaning, with blood beneath her on the floor. He cursed under his breath, because it was pretty obvious it was too late to move her to a birthing suite. He gave her knee a quick, reassuring pat. "It's going to be all right. I'm Dr. Moreno, and Ms. Cain is getting what we need to help you, okay?"

He shoved the desk against the wall then grabbed the chairs. As he carried them into the hallway to give them all room, he could see Gabby tearing toward him with a big bowl in her hands.

"Everything should be in here. Clamps, scissors, bulb suction, sutures. Syringe for delivering intramuscular Pitocin. Blankets."

"IV bag?"

"Yes."

He and Gabriella shared a look. It was clear she'd experienced this before, and also knew the potential hazards of delivering a baby under these conditions. A shriek of pain drew their attention to the patient, who was gasping and clutching her belly.

"I want…I want an epidural now."

"I'm afraid it's too late for that," Gabriella said in a gentle, soothing voice. "The baby's coming fast, Trina, but that's good news, because it won't hurt for long, right?"

"Then let's get the C-section done fast. But you can't do the C-section here, can you?" Trina sucked in a few heavy breaths. "I…I don't think I can walk. Can you get me moved to wherever you do that, maybe in a wheelchair?"

"C-section?" Gabriella glanced at Rafael with a question in her eyes, obviously asking if he'd somehow had a conversation with the woman about a Caesarean in the minute she'd been gone. He shook his head but since it was her patient kept quiet to let Gabriella handle it as she saw fit.

"Yes. I talked to my doctor about a C-section so I wouldn't have any changes in my, you know, down there, and he agreed."

"Trina, a vaginal birth is always preferable to a Caesarean section, both for the baby and for the amount of time your body needs to heal."

"I don't care. That's what I want. I know the scar would be low and not noticeable."

The mulish expression on her face contorted into pain as she had another long contraction. Rafael placed his hand on her belly. He could feel the muscles pushing hard, and was sure the baby was on its way. Gabriella must have thought the same thing, as she efficiently set up an IV line in the woman's arm.

Deciding that nature was making the decision for this woman about how her baby would be born, he figured an argument was unnecessary.

"Let's see how much you're dilated now, Trina," he said, giving her what he hoped was a comforting smile. "Do you want me to do the internal exam? Or would you prefer Ms. Cain to?"

"You, please," the woman gasped.

He glanced at Gabriella, and had a hard time not grinning at her narrowed eyes and the expression on her face that was just about the equivalent of her sticking her tongue out at him. But there was a twinkle in those eyes too so he knew she wasn't going to yell at him again.

He snapped on gloves and knelt in front of the woman. "All right. You'll feel a little pressure as I check. You're doing great." Gabriella got the IV taped down, then moved to hold one of Trina's knees.

Then their eyes met in surprise, and the plan changed again. Because the top of baby's head was clearly visible—as he'd guessed, nature had decided when this baby was going to be born. "Guess what, Mama? Baby's decided the time is now. We can see the top of its head. Push hard next time you have a contraction."

"Oh, God! No! I'm… I don't want it to be this way."

Gabby had turned to speak into the microphone around her neck, presumably to call Neonatal and get the troops ready, but now reached to squeeze Trina's hand as she moaned again. "I know, I'm sorry. But, ready or not, here he comes. Breathe now, it's going to be just fine. Give us a push, okay? Another one."

"Great job. Here he comes! I've got his head now." He

gently grasped the infant's head, sliding his fingers up to hold the tiny shoulders. "Another push."

As the mother labored, Gabriella kept up her encouragement. "You're doing an amazing job, Trina. Remember to breathe. Puff, puff, puff. One more. Oh, my, you've done it! He's here, and so beautiful!"

The baby was a good color and seemed to be under no stress at all, and the usual, spontaneous satisfaction hit Rafael square in the chest. He grinned at the mother then at Gabriella. Their eyes met for the briefest moment, but it was long enough to see she felt exactly like he did, which was that he wanted to pump his fists in the air that all had gone smoothly, despite the not-very-normal situation.

"You can be front-page news if you want to be, Trina," Gabriella said as she did a quick bulb suction on the baby before handing him to his mother. "I think you might be the first woman to give birth on the floor of the clinic midwife's office."

Trina, obviously tired but now beaming, laughed. "Being on the front page is always one of my goals."

Something Rafael couldn't imagine, and he'd be glad to have her take his place the next time it happened.

Neonatal arrived to take the baby and get him cleaned up and swaddled.

"Your body was obviously perfectly made for this, Trina, with baby coming so fast and easy, and with no complications at all." Rafael had learned that it was always good to distract his patients with chitchat and jokes while he took care of post-birth necessities. "You might consider doing it another ten times or so. What do you think?"

Predictably, Trina laughed at the same time she scowled at him. "Easy for you to say when you're not the one who went through the pain or got your body all stretched out. Besides, every woman's body is made for birthing babies, right? It's our curse in life, though I have to say he just might be worth it."

He smiled at the happy, adoring look she was giving her baby, then glanced at Gabriella, wanting to enjoy her smile, too.

Except she wasn't smiling. Her eyes held the sadness he'd seen in them before. No, this time he'd even call it anguish, and her slender shoulders were slumped with the weight of something heavy but invisible. Seeing her pain, that same heavy weight seemed to settle in his own chest as it ached for her, and he knew that, damn it, he had to learn what was making her feel this way.

To hell with keeping his distance. With keeping her safe from him. He might not have much to offer her other than the here and now and an ear to listen and a shoulder to cry on, but he could at least offer that. Or whatever it was she needed from him.

God knew, he was well acquainted with what it felt like to not have anyone close who particularly cared who you really were.

Dios. He wanted, right then, to take her in his arms and kiss away that sadness. To whisk her off somewhere to talk about it right now, to find out the source and show her that, whatever it was, it would be all right. Except they were at work, caring for a new mother and a new life. Waiting wasn't his strength, but patients had to come first.

Gabriella must have felt that he was watching her, maybe even sensed the intensity and turmoil inside him at that moment, because she turned to look at him. Their gazes fused for a long moment of charged connection before she blinked, then turned away. He saw a smile force its way to her lips as her face became a smooth mask. She chatted with Trina as she was helped onto a gurney to transport her to a room, and cooed over the baby the neonatal team had placed back in its mother's arms.

Anyone who hadn't been looking at Gabriella exactly when he had might have seen only the pleased, warm midwife caring for her patient. Giving them the kind of heartfelt attention and empathy any pregnant woman would be lucky to receive from her nurse.

Gabriella seemed to be pointedly directing her attention to anywhere and anyone but him as she and a technician got the room cleaned up. Just before the new mother was wheeled out, she thanked him and he turned to smile at her, chucking the little newborn under his chin but still thinking of Gabriella busying herself behind him. He pondered how exactly to approach her. His phone rang, and the screen told him it was James.

He stepped into the hallway, keeping an eye on Gabriella's office door to make sure she didn't escape before he had a chance to talk to her.

"Hello, James, what's up?"

"Can you take a couple of days to go to a special destination?" James asked.

"Depends on the destination."

"A sheikh friend and his wife and extended family are staying in Vail, Colorado. He came here to take care of some business in L.A., and they were planning to leave the U.S. day after tomorrow. Except it looks like she might be close to delivering earlier than expected. Any way you can head to the mountains to see what's going on?"

He didn't have to ask why they didn't just go to the local hospital or see a doctor there. He knew a number of Middle Eastern princes, and they didn't "do" local hospitals without having some connection, along with a guarantee of privacy.

"Any way they can get here?"

"No. He's worried, and doesn't want her to travel. So, can you?"

"Yes." For the first time in half an hour he felt like smiling. "Though I'd need assistance, which means you'll have to adjust Gabriella Cain's schedule so she can come with me."

"Those are your terms?" A low laugh came down the phone line. "Fine. But I hope you know what the hell you're doing, and why you're doing it."

Rafael wasn't too sure he knew either of those things, but he was going with it anyway.

CHAPTER NINE

SWOOPING DOWN THEN back up and around on the winding road that had been cut through sheer rock cliffs, the powerful rented sedan effortlessly handled the mountain curves Gabby was sure her own little car would have struggled with mightily. With any other driver at the wheel, she might have been a little nervous at the speed with which he was taking the sweeping turns, but Rafael's supreme confidence was evident, just like it was at work. Or anywhere else, for that matter.

She couldn't help but wonder if her coming along on this work trip had been James's idea or Rafael's. Somehow, she had a feeling it was the prince wielding his powers of persuasion, which was a nice way to say he was manipulative. But how could she be sorry about that?

She glanced at the man and his gorgeous profile, a smile playing at the corners of his mouth.

"Spectacular, isn't it, Gabriella?"

"Yes." And she wasn't about to tell him she was thinking of his looks as well as the scenery. "But I'm surprised you wanted to take the time to drive from the airport, instead of using a helicopter. I thought the Sheikh was worried to death."

"The chopper would only cut about twenty minutes off the trip. And I talked to both the Sheikh and his wife on the phone. Between you and me, I'm almost positive this is false labor, and maybe not even that. She's taking every twinge or odd feeling as something catastrophic. But of course we need to confirm that, which is why we're here."

Gabby stared out the window, suddenly not seeing the craggy rock cliffs and tumbling river below. She was remembering the odd twinges. Peculiar, off sensations that she too had assumed were nothing, focusing on her patient instead. A stupid error in judgment that had ended up being catastrophic indeed. "I hope we're seeing her as soon as we get there. Just in case."

"Don't worry. We are."

He must have sensed something in her response, because his voice had changed from pleased at enjoying their drive to more serious.

"If you think it's unlikely to be labor, why did you want me to come?"

"I don't know this man, and some sheikhs can be difficult to deal with. Traditional attitudes being what they are, it can be helpful to have a woman who's an experienced midwife helping care for his wife."

"I guess I can see that. How often has Dr. Jet-Setting OB run into problems with that?"

"A few times. When I do, I put on a wig and a dress. Solves everything."

He flashed her a quick grin, and Gabby laughed at that amusing and absurd vision. As though putting on those items would in any way disguise the potent masculinity that exuded from the man.

The road flattened and soon the wilderness gave way to houses and large apartment buildings alongside the highway, then the town of Vail itself came into view. Rafael swung the car through a roundabout and on into the village, where cobbled walks and charming buildings lined the streets, many designed to look like they belonged in an old Swiss town.

"Like I said, we'll stop at the hospital first, then check into the hotel."

Unable to shake the unease she felt about the pregnant woman's condition, Gabby was just about to ask how far it was to the hospital when she saw signs for it and they swung into the parking lot. "Wow, I'm surprised the hospital is so close to the main town. And how did you know where it was?"

"I've been here a few times. It's a good gig to combine skiing with working."

"I'd think you'd do that in Switzerland and Austria."

"There, too. Among other places. Like I said, it's a good gig." That grin again, then he was out of the car and coming over to her side to open the door, reaching for her hand.

"You don't have to open my door, you know. I'm an open-my-own-door kind of woman."

"Sorry if it bothers you. But as you noted the first day we met, I do as I please. And it pleases me to be a gentleman."

The words held a tinge of that arrogance that was just part of him, but his eyes were warm and sincere. Even as she rolled her eyes a little, she had to laugh. "I guess it's impossible for a prince to not believe he can do as he pleases. And since you haven't asked me to kiss your ring, I guess I'll indulge you by letting you assist me out of the car."

"The only reason I haven't asked you to kiss my ring is because I don't wear one. But I would like you to kiss something else." And with that, he leaned into the car and pressed his mouth to hers.

For a split second she stared into half-closed moss-green eyes before her own flickered shut. And just like that her heart began to pump in slow thuds as she savored the taste of him in her mouth, as she breathed in his scent, letting herself slowly sink into the kiss until he broke the delicious contact and pulled back.

The eyes staring at her this time had darkened, and it seemed his chest rose and fell in several deep breaths before his lip quirked at one corner. "Air's thin up here, isn't it? Let's go."

He held out his hand, and she didn't say a word as she slipped hers into it. Then kept it there as they walked into the hospital, and she had the same bad-good feeling she'd had when James had first told her she needed to come on this trip.

She'd never get truly involved with a man again. Never fully trust that kind of relationship. But if she had to briefly fall off that wagon, wasn't Rafael the perfect man to do it with? Okay, yes, she already had, figuring it would be just that one time. But she was beginning to see that, as long as he was still working at the clinic, there was no way she could resist letting their professional time together turn personal.

She wanted him. Again. And it looked like he wanted her the exact same way.

Her lips hadn't stopped tingling, and she willed herself to look normal as they stopped at the front desk to get directions to the seventh floor. Still holding her hand, he led her to the elevator. "I didn't hear what the room number was."

"That's because there's no need to know it. They've paid big money to basically rent out the whole floor."

"The whole floor?"

"Not uncommon. The Sheikh wants privacy and discretion. He'll likely have flown in his own staff to prepare food for everyone and to tend to his wife. Possibly brought comfortable furnishings for their stay here. I had one patient in Morocco whose family brought twelve place settings of fine china from their palace to the hospital."

"Wow." That was about the only thought she could conjure, though she wasn't sure if it was because she was so amazed or because her brain could only focus on one thing at a time, and at that moment it was still thinking about his lips and the feel of his hand wrapped around hers. About the rest of their stay here together and where it all might lead.

Rafael punched the elevator button and the doors closed. Alone in the enclosed space, their recent kiss sizzled in the air between them, so hot she could practically feel it burning her skin. And from the slight flare to his nostrils, the way his skin seemed to tighten over his cheekbones he felt every bit as much heat as she did.

The elevator pinged open just in time, since her fantasy of grabbing him and pushing him back against the wall to have her way with him was making her feel a little woozy. Their eyes met, and she saw his lips curved in a half-smile and realized hers were, too. Then he gave her a quick wink, and it was so unexpected from autocratic Prince Rafael Moreno she gave a little breathless laugh.

"We'll hold that thought until later, hmm, *bella*?" he murmured.

They walked down the corridor, and Gabby couldn't help but stare at the number of people around. Some wore uniforms, and others were dressed in elegant clothes. There were even quite a few children, and while some occupied themselves quietly with a board game, several boys were tearing down the hall, kicking a ball and shouting.

"This looks like a hospital, and yet not," she said to Rafael in disbelief. "Does the hospital director know this is going on?"

"I'm willing to bet he's done this drill once or twice so, yes. Also planned ahead and put away any equipment that could be damaged by an errant kick." His eyes twinkled. "Let's see how our patient is doing. I'll find out where she is."

He stepped toward a small group of women and started speaking in some language Gabby had never heard, amazed at him and his various skills. Though she shouldn't have been, really. Probably a prince grew up learning any number of languages. She felt embarrassed all over again at her very rudimentary knowledge of Spanish, vowing to study it more. She hadn't needed it too much in Seattle, but speaking the language even halfway well would come in very handy in California.

"This way," Rafael said. He didn't lead the way, having her follow. Instead, he waited for her to join him, then pressed his hand against her lower back as they walked together.

"More of your gentlemanliness? Waiting for me?" she teased.

"Or maybe I just wanted an excuse to touch you."

The gaze that met hers was twinkling, but hot, too, and Gabby sank her teeth into her lower lip to make sure nothing came out that shouldn't. Something along the lines of *You don't need an excuse, which I'm pretty sure you know.*

Acutely aware of that wide hand on her back, she had to wonder when she'd gone from being an efficient workaholic uninterested in dating to a woman with sex on her mind in the middle of a hospital. Though she knew the answer, and it was standing right next to her in all its six-foot-plus gorgeous glory.

When they went into the patient's room, Gabby was in for yet another unexpected sight. The place looked more like a plush hotel room than a hospital room. Even more so than The Hollywood Hills Clinic rooms—and, since she'd always thought they seemed right out of a five-star hotel, that was saying something. This had to be one of those situations Rafael mentioned where they'd brought in furniture for their stay. A portable wall between two rooms had been removed, creating a huge space, and comfortable furniture filled the area. The bed was still a hospital bed, but it had beautiful linens, and the bedspread looked like something from a high-end furnishings magazine.

An exotic-looking woman lay in the bed, which surprised Gabby a little. Since she wasn't connected to any monitors or IV at this point, Gabby would have expected her to be sitting in one of the deep, upholstered armchairs, but maybe she felt more comfortable lying down. Or maybe, since Rafael had said her husband was worried, everyone thought she should stay in the bed to be safe.

Rafael made introductions, then focused his attention on speaking with the Sheikh, which also surprised Gabby. Normally, getting information and history directly from the patient was important, but since Rafael knew that, it must be part of the typical protocol in this very atypical situation. Maybe this was exactly why he'd wanted her to come, so she could speak directly to the patient without going through her husband first. If she spoke English, that was.

Of course, she couldn't deny that she hoped Rafael had wanted her along for another reason, too. Then scolded herself for having that sex subject dive back into her mind when she had work to do.

"Hello, Amala, I'm Gabby Cain, a nurse midwife from The Hollywood Hills Clinic. I understand you're having some pain, and are worried about the baby?"

"Yes." Thankfully, Amala spoke excellent English, and

Gabby smiled in relief. “I keep having pains. Contractions, I think.”

“Have you timed them at all? To see how far apart they are?”

“No. But they happen often.”

“Okay. I’m going to take your pulse and blood pressure to check those—is that all right?” She pressed her fingers to the woman’s delicate wrist. “Tell me about the pain. Where is it, exactly?”

“My belly. Low. And down…there as well.”

The woman seemed uncomfortable even using a euphemism, and Gabby smiled wider to hopefully relax her. “The good news is that your pulse and blood pressure are normal. So, are you feeling any pain in your back? Up high in your belly?”

“No. Not my back. I am not sure about how high. But they go away sometimes if I lie down.”

Sounded like Rafael might be right about this being false labor, but it was too soon to say for sure. She glanced up to see him finishing his conversation with the Sheikh, then he came to join her on the other side of the patient’s bed.

“I’m Dr. Rafael Moreno. It’s my privilege to come see you today. I understand you’re thirty-four weeks pregnant. Can you tell me about your symptoms?”

Amala repeated what she’d told Gabby, and more as he asked additional questions. Finally, he nodded. “Let’s take a look at what baby is doing inside you, using ultrasound. You have it ready, Gabriella?”

“Yes.”

“Good.” He reached to lift the patient’s shirt over her belly, but she stopped him.

“I’d like Gabriella to do it. Please.”

The surprise on his face was gone in a blink, replaced

by a calm smile. "Of course. Gabriella is excellent with ultrasound, and I can read them later as well, if you want. I'll be back in a little bit."

His gaze lifted from their patient and his eyes met Gabby's. She absolutely could not control the gleeful little smile quivering on her lips that the tide had turned, and this time the patient trusted her to do the job instead of him.

Gabby slowly ran the wand through the warm jelly she'd squeezed on Amala's abdomen, and carefully studied the pictures on the monitor. Seeing that everything looked one hundred percent normal, and that baby seemed healthy in every way, Gabby's knees got a little jelly-like, too, as relief for the woman swept through her. "Baby looks absolutely perfect in there, all snug and happy. I'm going to go over my findings with Dr. Moreno, but I'm confident that the pain you've been experiencing is false labor, which can be very hard to distinguish from true labor."

"Oh, I hope so. I want my baby to be born at home, so this is good news. Thank you so much."

"So glad to be here to help you." And she was. Glad, in a strange kind of way, that she knew exactly how this pregnant woman had felt, which made her a better caregiver. A better nurse and midwife. She cleaned off the gel and got the patient's top back in place. "Let me see what Dr. Moreno thinks, okay?"

She found him sitting at a round table, playing the board game with the kids there, all of them laughing. Struck by how boyish he looked, too, so unlike the arrogant prince or the dashing date, she slowed her steps and just looked at him, her heart feeling all warm and squishy and starstruck.

He glanced up and grinned at her. Unfolding himself from the chair, he came over to her. "False labor?"

"Yes." She cleared her throat and went over the results

with him, and for the first time in her professional life a tiny corner of her mind was on something other than her patient and her work. It was on him, and the scent of him, and how close his head was tipped to hers. Afraid everyone in the room could see how she was feeling and what she was thinking, she again went for a joke to cover it all.

"So, Dr. Prince Rafael Moreno, how does it feel to have your patient doubt your skills and send you out of the room, leaving someone else to do the tests?"

"First, she did not doubt my skills. I'm sure she just knew her husband might be jealous because I am so handsome."

The gold flecks sparkling in his green eyes showed he was teasing, and didn't believe that for a minute. Probably it had been more about modesty, but Gabby was going to rib him about it anyway.

"Uh-huh. All I can say is it made me pretty happy for you to get a taste of it, considering how mean you were the first day we met."

"Mean?" All humor left his face as he looked at her searchingly. "You thought I was mean? I'm sorry if that's how I came across."

"Okay, mean isn't the right word." A man as empathetic as he was didn't have a mean bone in his body. "Dismissive. Disrespectful."

"And for that I apologize too. Only a fool would disrespect or dismiss someone like you, and sometimes the fool in me comes out when it shouldn't."

"Never mind." Lord, she'd meant it really as a joke, and now he looked so contrite, ashamed, even, she was sorry she'd even mentioned it. Who would have thought the man was even capable of feeling that way? "I'm teasing you, really. Like you do me sometimes."

"I know exactly how to make it up to you in about..."

he glanced at his watch "…half an hour. Let's talk to the Sheikh and his wife, hmm?"

Walking beside him, she couldn't help but glance up at him more than once, wondering what he'd meant about making it up to her, and her toes and a lot of other things started to tingle as she imagined what it could be.

You're at work, Gabby! she scolded herself. And work was not the place where her mind could be wandering to bad thoughts.

She stood on the opposite side of the patient's bed as Rafael recommended they stay one more day. He told Amala to write down when she had contractions and how long they lasted, and to be ready for Gabby to do one more ultrasound tomorrow. Gabby tried to listen, but since she knew everything he was going to say, watching his lips move seemed far more fascinating. As did wondering what in the world he had in mind to "make it up" to her.

Those darned thoughts of sex came right to the forefront of her brain again. When in the world was that going to stop?

Probably only after Rafael Moreno was long gone back to the Mediterranean or wherever he was headed next. Her life could get back to normal. The life she'd chosen where she worked a lot and stayed relationship-free. Since it was apparent that she couldn't seem to help but be dangerously distracted by him, she knew that day couldn't come soon enough.

Yet she also had a bad feeling it would also come far, far too soon.

CHAPTER TEN

ADVENTURES IN THE sky were nothing new to Rafael. He'd enjoyed hang gliding, glider planes, and skydiving many times all over the world. At the time, he'd thought every one of those adventures was enjoyable, but nothing came close to the evening he'd just spent with Gabriella.

Holding her close as they'd stood in the basket of a hot-air balloon, able to see for miles across the awesome expanse of the Rocky Mountains, they'd floated through a quiet so deep he'd felt it all the way to his soul. Filled with a tranquil contentment he couldn't remember ever feeling in his life.

Listening to her cries of delight as she'd pointed at beautiful blue-green lakes below, at the snow still covering the jagged peaks, at mountain goats picking their way across vertical rocks in a feat that seemed nearly impossible, he'd smiled and laughed and held her closer.

Her hair had blown across her face, and he'd tucked it behind her ears more than once, both to feel its softness within his fingers and so he could better see the joy on her face and in her eyes.

Joy he'd wanted to see there from the moment he'd observed them shadowed with sadness when she'd sat next to Skye's incubator. Joy he'd known was a big part of who she was, or had been until something had chipped away at it. Minimized it. Maybe even crushed it.

As the balloon had sunk back to earth, they'd watched the sun set in a blaze of glorious red and gold behind the mountains. Colors so vivid they'd almost rivaled the strands highlighting Gabriella's beautiful hair.

He'd wanted to have her to himself for a little while longer, away from L.A. and whatever was there that might be the reason she carried that sadness around. Again, he knew that was damned selfish of him, but he'd been having a tough time battling it. And since fate had seemed to give him exactly what he'd wanted, did he really have to fight it?

All he knew was that he didn't seem to have a lot of fight left in him when it came to keeping away from Gabriella.

He opened the door of the hotel restaurant, sliding his hand around hers before they meandered out onto the huge stone patio, warmed by several fire pits surrounded by cushioned chairs. And, lucky for him, it was nearly deserted.

"Would you like to sit out here? Or are you too full to sit after you ate a steak big enough for two people?" he couldn't help but tease.

"Haven't we already discussed how not at all suave it is to talk about how much I eat?" Her eyes gleamed up at him. "All women need iron in their diets. The occasional steak is good for me. But I'm not sure what your excuse is, because you ate even more than I did."

"Fresh out of excuses." That was true for pretty much anything he did around Gabriella, and he didn't care anymore. "Where would you like to sit?"

"By the fire. It's getting chilly, don't you think?"

"We can go inside if you like."

"No. It's so beautiful, I want to stay out here." He followed her gaze over to the timeless mountains, silhouetted by the darkened sky that was still slightly lit with pale pink streaks. Across the creek covered with small chunks of ice and snow, slowly melting in the springtime temperatures. "I can't believe there's no one around to enjoy this."

"May is off season for Vail. Too late to ski and too cold for most other sports."

"Except hot-air ballooning. Bundling up in a ski coat, gloves and hat were part of the fun." Her eyes smiled at him through the darkness. "And since I don't even own a coat, it's a good thing the hotel keeps winter stuff guests have left behind for people like me to borrow."

"I'm sure you're not the only Southern Californian to come here unprepared."

"Unprepared?" He nearly laughed at her indignant expression. "I was a Girl Scout. Believe me, I know how to be prepared."

"If you say so. How about we sit here?" He tugged her down to a thickly pillowed settee, and he could feel the warmth of the fire reaching out to him. Much like Gabriella's warmth did, touching him in ways he couldn't remember being touched before. "I'm glad you liked it."

"I loved it. It was the most special thing I've ever done. Thank you."

"The most special thing I've done too. So thank you." And the reason it had been so special was because he'd done it with her. How he felt about her was something he couldn't quite figure out, but he suspected that feeling might not happen again for a long time. Or maybe ever.

"I know that can't be true, but it's sweet of you to say so." She laughed softly. "You've been all over the world, but I haven't left L.A. in two years."

"You haven't?" He couldn't wrap his brain around not getting out of town even once in all that time. "That's got to be a record. I haven't *stayed* in one place more than two months since I graduated from medical school."

"Yours is more likely to be a record than mine."

He saw her shiver a little in the crisp mountain air, despite the orange flames licking upward, ending in gray smoke that disappeared into the starlit sky. He wrapped his arm around her shoulders and tugged her close to his side, and the way she snuggled against him felt damn good. "Cold?"

"A little. My Washington State blood, used to damp, chilly weather, must have thinned after living in California."

"I've been wanting to ask you something." If she was feeling even a little of the closeness, the intimacy he was feeling right now, sitting next to her in this beautiful place, maybe now was the right time to learn what secrets she might be keeping to herself. Secrets she might need to unload.

"What?"

"I've noticed that sometimes when you look at newborns, or after you've helped bring a baby into the world, that there's a sadness in your eyes. Why?"

"Sadness?" She made a sound that was probably supposed to be a laugh but didn't get there. "I don't know what you're talking about. There's nothing more joyful than a successful delivery and healthy baby, and you know it."

"But sometimes a pregnancy doesn't end successfully. Or with a healthy baby," he said quietly, his gut telling him there was some kind of history for her that was tied to that reality.

"True."

She stared fixedly at the fire, her relaxed expression more tense now. He hesitated, wondering if asking her more questions would ruin her evening. And his too. But he'd wanted to provide an ear in case she wanted to unload on him, so he'd try just once more. "Why did you leave Seattle to come to L.A.?"

More staring into the fire, and just when he was regretting ruining the intimate comfort they'd been feeling by digging into her life, instead of keeping it light and superficial like he usually did, she sighed and started to talk.

"I was engaged to be married. Thought I had it all—a job I adored, a family who supported me, a man who loved me. But it turned out he didn't love me, at least not enough. Something…bad happened, and he left me. I decided to start fresh in L.A., and that's it in a nutshell."

He wanted to say that any man who had her in his life, planning on forever, then left was a fool and an idiot. But he knew that was just the way relationships turned out most of the time. Unfortunate for people who believed in that kind of love, but it was reality. Either someone left, or a couple stuck together long past the time they should have gone their separate ways.

Her boyfriend's abandonment, causing her pain, was just more proof that relationships weren't meant to last for the long haul, and that planning to get married was just a road leading to unhappiness.

"I'm sorry. That must have been hard for you."

"It was. But I'm over it now."

Somehow he didn't believe that. But he knew her well enough to know she was done talking about it, even though he was sure it couldn't be the whole story. He slipped his fingers beneath her chin, tipping her face up to his, and all he could think of to do for her was kiss away the sadness on her face, replacing it with the desire he'd seen there on and off all day. Desire that he'd battled with a whole lot of effort, because he didn't want to hurt her. A battle he had to win now that he knew her ex had already caused her pain.

But just as he was about to draw back and start some unimportant chitchat, she wrapped her cold hand around his nape, brought his face close, and pressed her mouth to his.

He could see her eyes closing just before his own did, and the way she sighed and sank into him knocked every good intention out of his head and had him gathering her close. He cupped her soft cheek in his hand, angling her mouth to his, and when she sighed again it felt like a siren song, driving him a little crazy. He couldn't help but deepen the kiss. The wet slide of her warm tongue against his felt as erotic as full sex with any other woman, and it was only through some miracle that he managed to remember that, deserted or not, they were in a public place and pulling off her clothes right then and there wasn't an option.

Or a good idea. He absolutely was not going to be the next man to hurt her.

"Gabriella." He sucked in some much-needed air. "It's too cold out here to be comfortable. Let's go inside and talk in the lounge."

"I'm very comfortable."

Well, damn. What was he supposed to say to that? She pressed her chest to his, and while he couldn't really feel her breasts against him, knowing what softness lay under all the layers of clothes they wore nearly made him moan. Her cold hands cupped his cheeks and she brought his face to hers again for another mind-blowing kiss that had him thinking about risking arrest and getting naked with her right there after all. Thank God the murmur of other voices on the patio cut through his fog and helped him get his libido at least marginally in check.

Which then helped him remember the paparazzi and how he needed to keep Gabriella safe from the media.

While he hoped they hadn't gotten wind of them coming to Vail, he'd learned not to count on that.

He dragged his lips from hers and sucked in a deep breath of chilly mountain air that barely cooled the heat pouring through his veins. "Bad idea to do this out here. Cameras, you know?"

The brown eyes that met his looked a little dazed, but she nodded. "Cameras. I remember. How about we go to the room?"

Knowing she wanted that, too, made what he had to say nearly impossible. But he forced himself. "Gabriella, it's better if—"

"Stop." She pressed her fingertips to his lips. "You asked me things. There are things I want to ask you too."

He braced himself, not being in the mood for true confessions. Mostly because he hated to see her shock and disappointment and disapproval. But she probably had a right to know.

"Ask away."

"Why are you hiding out in L.A.?"

"What makes you think I'm hiding? I'm visiting."

"I don't live under a rock, Rafael. I know there was a scandal with some woman."

The way she smiled and cupped his cheek in her hand relaxed him a little. At least she knew that much, and was still there with him. He turned his face to press his mouth to her palm for a moment, deciding what he wanted to say.

"Then you know I dated a woman who some people thought was not the kind of person a prince should be dating. It wasn't as though we had anything more than a casual relationship, but the media hounds ran with it, as they love to do. Since my face had been plastered on television and tabloids quite a lot the past couple years, there was more uproar than usual back home."

"Do you care about it? And if you do, why do you do things you know the media will have a field day with?"

At first, he thought she was judging him, and the pain of that stabbed his chest. But when he looked into her eyes, really looked, he could clearly see that she was just asking, not judging. Her hand still softly caressed his cheek, and the touch weakened him. Or made him stronger, he wasn't sure which. Either way, he realized he actually wanted to talk to her about it, which surprised the hell out of him.

He drew in a fortifying breath before he spoke. "First, half the stuff said about me isn't true. Or is greatly exaggerated. Second, if I read that stuff and worried about it, I'd spend all day doing it and I have more important things to think about."

"So why hide out at all?"

Good question, and one he wasn't sure how to answer. "My parents get upset about it. And this time the hubbub was so loud they demanded I lie low and keep my face out of the press. And since I'm a grown man and can do as I please, my only explanation of why I did so is that I care about their opinion of me. Because their opinion's been pretty low for a long time, and I guess that's always bothered me."

His words rang in his ears, and it was like being given a good whack on the side of the head. Apparently there was some part of him deep inside that was still that boy who was the second prince. The spare heir. The one who didn't always follow rules and had embarrassed his parents when he'd left the kingdom to become a doctor. The one who refused to ever marry, despite having very good reasons for that.

The son they were always disappointed in, whether he lived up or down to his reputation in the media. Pathetic that it hurt that they felt that way, but there it was. The truth.

"What do you mean, their opinion of you is low? That's ridiculous."

"Not ridiculous." He pressed his lips to her forehead and let them stay there, because the simple connection felt good. "I told you before that they wanted me to stay in the family business, so to speak. They never understood or approved of my wanting to be a doctor, and were more than disappointed when I did it anyway."

"Rafael." She grasped his face in her hands, and he felt a little like he was drowning in the sweet sincerity of the brown eyes staring into his. "I don't know your parents. But I have to believe you're wrong about a lot of this. Maybe they wanted you to do more traditional duties at home, but surely they're proud of the hard work you put in to be a doctor. Of the lives you save and the good you do. When you go home, promise me you'll talk to them. Share how you've felt, and clear the air. I bet you'll be surprised at how they respond."

Gabriella knew a lot about human nature—hadn't he seen it first hand in so many ways? That didn't mean she knew a thing about his family situation, but he realized he didn't have anything to lose by talking things over with his parents. Who knew, maybe they could come up with a relationship less full of stress and more full of the kind of closeness he'd seen in other families. Including royal ones like those of the Sheikh they'd met today, who obviously cared deeply about his extended family.

"I don't expect anything would change, but for you I'll think about it."

"Not for me, for you. Because after another week or so we won't see each other again."

A good thing for her. Not so much for him. She was the most special woman he'd ever known, and he wished they could spend more time together. But he was a man who generally disappointed the people in his life, and she was a woman who'd already been badly disappointed by someone else. She deserved someone who believed in love and happy-ever-after. He definitely didn't, but maybe she'd somehow find that one day.

The thought made his chest feel oddly tight and he stood to end the torture of being with her when he shouldn't be. "We have an early morning. The Sheikh wants to get going as soon as we check once more that his wife's not in labor."

Her gaze stayed on his as she slowly pushed to her feet. Searching. Questioning. Not a surprise, since moments ago he'd been kissing her like a man on a mission to get horizontal with her as soon as possible.

Much as he still wanted that more than his next breath, she deserved better.

They walked in silence to their rooms, which were connected by an interior door, and Rafael knew he wouldn't get much sleep, thinking about her warm, soft body curled into a bed so close to his. The same way he'd been unable to sleep the night he'd tucked her into the guest room of his house, and he hadn't even known her then.

Now that he did, now that he knew the attraction was mutual, staying away from her would require Herculean strength, but for her sake he could do it.

Stopping at the door to her room, he somehow managed to kiss only her cheek, though he knew his lips lingered there too long. "Good night, Gabriella."

"This is totally unfair, you know."

"What is totally unfair?"

"Getting James to include me on this trip, then making me sit close to you, look at you, feel the touch of your hand while we drove, and it was all so distracting I barely noticed the gorgeous scenery. Then you took me on a romantic balloon ride with your arms around me, which was the most incredible thing I've ever done. More romance and kissing and touching by a fire under the stars. And now you dump me like a hot rock in front of my door?"

The flash of fire in her eyes, the annoyance in her voice and her words were so surprising and adorable he couldn't help but laugh, even though having to leave her now wasn't in the least amusing. "Dumping is a strong word. I'm simply dropping you off after a wonderful day together."

"Why?" A challenge in her brown eyes joined that single word.

"For the reasons we just talked about outside, Gabriella," he said quietly, hoping she'd understand. "You deserve so much more than someone like me can give you. I'm leaving soon, and I don't want to be another man who disappoints you."

"You can't disappoint me if I'm not expecting anything." Her fingers slid up the front of his jacket to grasp his neck again, on up to trace his jaw and cheekbones, and even that simple touch made him want her even more. "You've made me see that I've been living in a cocoon this past two years. Hiding. But unlike you've had to do in these past weeks, I haven't been hiding from outside forces. Haven't been hiding because someone asked me to. I've been hiding from myself, and now I know it's time to change that." Her eyes softened, and her voice dropped to a whisper. "Being with you tonight is all I want. Breaking out of my shell to enjoy just one more incredible night with an incredible man. Is that so much to ask?"

He didn't even realize he'd wrapped his arms around her until his hold tightened and he couldn't make himself let her go. He warred with himself about the right thing to do. "Gabriella—"

She rose on tiptoe and buried her hands in his hair.

Pulled his mouth to hers for a kiss so long and sweet and hot it fried every last working brain cell he had left.

He somehow broke the kiss and stared into her beautiful eyes. "You promise you won't regret it when I leave? That you won't feel hurt that I can't stay?"

"I won't regret it. I won't be hurt. Unless you walk away this second. In which case I'll have to become like autocratic Rafael Moreno was the first day we met and 'take control of the situation.'"

How a woman's eyes could be amused, sensual, and flashing all at the same time he had no idea, but it was an irresistible combination. He loved how Gabriella made him smile and laugh and want her so much he ached. "You already know I hate to give up control of any situation, *mi ángel*," He touched his mouth to hers and began to walk her backwards ten feet down the hallway to his own door. "So how about we take control of it together?"

"I like that idea a lot."

And with that she plastered her body close to his, wrapped her arms around his neck and kissed him, which was so distracting he had a hard time remembering in which pocket he'd stuffed his room key. "Can you wait for just two seconds while I find my key?"

"I don't know. But I'm happy to help you look."

She peppered kisses on his face at the same time she put her hand caressingly into his pants pocket, obviously looking for something other than his room key, and he laughed then nearly moaned.

"I'd never have dreamed that charming midwife Gabriella Cain could be such a vixen." Thank God he finally found the key in his jacket pocket, because she was driving him crazy and they were both still fully clothed. He shoved the door open and nearly stumbled as he backed her inside because now that they weren't in a public hallway and he'd abandoned all worries of hurting her, he couldn't get his hands and mouth on her fast enough.

"I've never been a vixen, I don't think." She pushed his jacket off at the same time he was unzipping hers. "Apparently, you bring her out in me."

"I'm about to show you what you bring out in me. Didn't you say you felt like Cinderella at the charity ball? I think I may be turning into the Beast." And while it was a joke, it wasn't far from the truth. He'd already stripped off her sweater and was in the process of unbuttoning her pants, and couldn't remember a time he'd felt as desperate to make love with a woman as he felt right now.

"You're mixing up your fairy tales. But since you are a prince, I guess that's okay."

She lost him on the conversation because he'd gotten her pants off and he took a moment to look at her, holding his breath at the vision before him. At her slim body, her luminous eyes, her hair a little tousled and her beautiful lips parted. He reached to unclasp her bra and as she stood there in near-naked perfection, he felt humbled. Incredibly lucky to be the man she'd chosen to break out of her shell with.

"Gabriella." He drew her close and kissed her, drinking in the taste of her and the sweetness of her, then scooped her up against his chest. A couple of steps to the bed and he'd deposited her in it, stripping off the last of his clothes to slide in next to her, loving the feel of her skin against his.

He captured her wrists in his hands and raised them above her head, letting his other roam in a gentle touch over her breasts and down her ribs as his mouth captured her nipple.

"I guess you were serious about taking control." She gasped. "How can I touch you if you're holding my hands?"

"Later. First, I want to make you feel good." So good,

so special for her that she'd never feel regret. Just memories of what it had been like between them, which he knew he'd never forget.

He moved his mouth back to hers, slipping his hand between her legs to feel the wetness there, caressing her for long minutes, and with any other woman he might have joined with her right then. But this was Gabriella, and he wanted to touch her all night. Could listen to her little moans forever as she writhed and gasped, but finally her hands broke free of his hold and she reached for him.

"I thought we agreed we were going to share control tonight, hmm?" she said, grasping and stroking him until he was the one moaning.

"Take pity on me, *bella.* The truth is I have little control around you."

He could feel her smile against his lips. "That's what I like to hear, Dr. Moreno. And remember how I said I was a Girl Scout? Always prepared?"

He laughed when he saw she had a condom in her hand, and where she'd grabbed it from he had no clue. Didn't care either, because after she slid it in place she rose up and sheathed herself on him. Rafael had never seen anything so beautiful in his life as this woman moving gracefully above him, looking down at him through eyes shining with the same intense desire that clawed into his very soul, leaving him weak. He held her hips, moving faster, wanting to see her expression as she came undone. When she did, arching her back and crying out, he was again filled with awe that he'd been privileged enough to be the one to put that look of ecstasy on her face. Then he followed her with his own cry of rapture as he gathered her close to his pounding heart. A heart he knew would never be quite the same again.

* * *

Rafael awoke to the feel of a slender shoulder pressed against his collarbone and a round, firm bottom spooned against him, and instantly began to harden at the sweet sensations and memories of last night's incredible lovemaking. Never had he experienced something so beyond the physical with a woman. Something that had demanded engagement from his heart and mind and soul every bit as much as his body.

He softly kissed Gabriella's hair, the hair he so loved to look at and touch. The golden fire that was such a part of who she was both inside and out, feisty and angelic, determined and dazzling. He moved his lips to the soft curve behind her ear, which he'd learned was a sweet spot she particularly enjoyed him kissing, but she didn't stir. Apparently she felt as worn out by their time together as he did. Worn out by the emotion of sharing their secrets with one another as much as their late-night lovemaking.

Finally hearing her story about her ex had been satisfying. Not completely, because he had a feeling there was more to the story than she'd wanted to talk about last night. But knowing she'd trusted him enough to share at least part of the reason she confessed she'd hidden away the past two years felt good. He wanted to be the person she danced with in the sunlight now that she'd decided to come out to play.

But he couldn't be that person, couldn't risk hurting her, and that reality blasted his sense of triumph to smithereens. He wouldn't be here for her. Couldn't be her forever love, because such a thing didn't exist.

He tucked her warm, captivating body closer, closing his eyes to breathe her in, and the ache in his chest told him one thing for certain. At least one person would hurt like hell when he moved on from L.A., and it would be the first time in his life that ending a fling would make him feel anything but guilt or relief.

The muffled tones of his cellphone had him searching for it in the bed, finally finding it when he slid his hand beneath Gabriella's pillow. This time she did stir, and his good morning murmur in her ear got cut off in mid-word when he saw who was calling.

His brother.

What could he possibly want? His brother's life was full of responsibilities that Rafael was more than happy to not have. Also more than happy that his brother rarely called, because when he did it was usually to scold him for embarrassing the royal family, as if it wasn't enough to hear it from both his mother and his father.

He nearly ignored the call, but finally swung his feet to the side of the bed and stood, striding to the bathroom so as not to disturb Gabriella. "To what do I owe the honor, Alberto?"

"Unfortunately, I have bad news. Mother has had a heart attack, and you need to come home right away."

CHAPTER ELEVEN

GABBY DID HER best to focus on work but, despite repeatedly yanking her attention back to her job, she kept making silly mistakes. Thankfully none had been too important, but still. How often did she normally drop things? When was the last time she'd walked into the storage room before completely forgetting what she'd needed? It had happened twice already. And giving a patient still water when she'd asked for sparkling...? Never.

And she knew it was because Rafael and his family were weighing on her mind. When he'd told her he had to leave and why, he'd sounded very matter-of-fact, but she knew him now. Knew that behind that suave and confident exterior was a man with a sensitive heart who cared passionately for others. No matter what he'd said about his family, about his conviction that they were disappointed in him, that he'd let them down when he'd decided to take a different path than what they'd planned for him, she could see he wasn't indifferent to it. That he cared about that more than he'd ever let on. And when she'd looked into his eyes after he'd told her his mother was ill, the calm mask on his face hadn't concealed the worry in his eyes.

Of course he'd been worried. No matter what kind of relationship anyone had with their parents, they were still important. Still loved.

She stared, unseeing, at the tray of supplies in her hands. Love. Such a complicated and confusing thing. She'd been so sure she'd loved Ben, had made a baby with him and had been planning to marry him. But now? Now she knew the truth. That it had all just been easy. They'd dated, he'd seemed like a good, stable man, and when she'd gotten pregnant had figured it was time to get married. Wasn't that what most people would have done?

But she'd never really loved him.

She knew that now. Knew because she was crazily in love with Rafael Moreno. Arrogant prince, excellent doctor, and tender lover. The knowledge balled her stomach, and her heart swelled at the same time it pinched tight. How had she let herself fall in love with the man? A notorious playboy, an international jet-setter who didn't stay in one place very long, and a man who freely admitted he didn't believe in forever-after love.

Truth was, though, she couldn't blame herself. It hadn't been a question of letting herself fall for him. It would have been like trying to stop an ocean wave as she swam in the Pacific, because Rafael was a force of nature every bit as mesmerizing and powerful.

She loved him. And when he'd kissed her goodbye, she'd known there was a good chance he might never be back.

The ball in her stomach rolled and her knuckles whitened on the tray, but she lifted her chin as she picked up her pace down the hallway. Somehow she had to focus on what she did best, which was work. It wasn't Rafael's fault she'd fallen so hard for him. If he called to report back about his mother, which he'd promised to do, she'd do everything in her ability to listen like a friend would and not let him know how much she missed him. How much she hoped he'd come back to L.A., but at the same time part of her hoped he wouldn't.

The love, the connection she felt with him seemed huge and overwhelming and uncontrollable. But the thought of having a real relationship with someone again? Something more than the short fling she'd decided to allow herself with him? Just the idea of it scared her to death.

"Why do I even care, Freya?"

Gabby hesitated at the sound of Mila's upset voice, not wanting to walk by the open lounge door while she was obviously having a personal conversation. "He already broke my heart once—shouldn't that have been enough to make my feelings turn to stone where he's concerned?"

"We can't just turn our feelings on and off like a faucet, Mila," Freya said in a soothing tone. "It's okay to feel the way you do."

"I mean, it almost seems like he's flaunting his new girlfriend, doesn't it? Like he's deliberately waving her in my face to upset me."

"I think James...well, he might be having his own struggles, Mila. He's never been one to let emotions control him, you know? Maybe his behavior is some unconscious reaction to seeing you again. I don't know what else to say, except you should tell him what you just told me and give him some time to think about it."

Now tearful, Mila continued to talk, and Gabby pivoted, deciding to go back the other way so as not to embarrass her. Her already aching heart hurt a little more, feeling bad that Mila was so upset. Why did life have to be so hard? Why did love have to hurt?

Giving your heart to someone made you horribly vulnerable, she knew. So where, exactly, did that leave her when it came to Dr. Rafael Moreno?

* * *

Everyone walking the hospital hallways drifted toward the walls to leave an open path as Rafael strode through, murmuring to one another and bowing as he passed, and his lips twisted at the sure sign he was home. He'd grown up with that kind of deference. Hadn't really even noticed it until he'd left the country. Now most people just saw him as a doctor, and it struck him how much he greatly preferred that to this kind of respect, based only on his birthright and not his accomplishments.

Something his parents and brother still didn't understand.

He pressed his lips together and forged on until he got to his mother's room. Then surprised himself when he had to stop outside it to inhale long calming breaths, fighting for composure. It wasn't as though he didn't practically live in hospitals. Between medical school and residency and working around the world, doing basic medicine and not the specialized obstetrics he did elsewhere, he'd seen thousands of sick people. Had seen plenty of them die. Had seen patients make miraculous recoveries too.

But none of them had been his mother.

Yes, she aggravated him, insulted him, berated him and lectured him. But she was still his mother and, damn it, he loved her. She'd been so angry about the recent press brouhaha and the various photos and lurid details, half of which had been made up, and he wasn't proud of the things he'd said back to her when she'd scolded him about it. He couldn't remember what they were, exactly, but he knew his words had hurt her feelings.

All that felt pretty unforgivable now that she was lying in a hospital bed in Intensive Care. Even though her heart attack had been fairly mild and the prognosis was good, he also knew things could go downhill fast.

Bracing himself, he forced his feet to go through the doorway. Then stood feeling slightly off balance at the end of the hospital bed, gripping the railing tight, because the pale woman hooked up to machines, with an I.V. in her arm and an oxygen hose in her nose, didn't look like his mother at all. She looked a good ten years older than the last time he'd seen her, and in that very second he vowed to never let so much time go by again between visits.

He swallowed hard then looked past the scary things to the one thing that seemed normal and familiar. Her hair was remarkably well coiffed and tidy for someone lying in the ICU after a heart attack, and it helped him manage a smile. Yes, this woman was his mother after all. The vain queen of the land who was always perfect and regal from head to toe.

Her eyelids flickered open and took a moment to focus on him. Then she smiled and slowly extended her hand. "Rafael."

The heavy tightness in his chest loosened at the way she said his name. At the way her smile, weak as it was, lit her tired eyes. He quickly stepped around the bed to grasp her hand. "Hi, Mother. Your hair looks nice. I'm surprised, though, that you're not wearing lipstick."

Her smile widened into a slightly wheezy chuckle. "Had one tucked under my pillow, but I think the nurse took it when they changed the sheets." The squeeze she gave his hand was weak but stronger than he'd expected, and he began to relax.

"Isn't this a rather drastic way to get me to come home?"

"You make me do drastic things. You've been like that since you were a little boy, and you're apparently never going to change, even if it kills me."

"And apparently you aren't going to change either, scolding me while flat on your back in a hospital bed."

Her acerbic tone was that of the queen and mother he knew well, but her eyes held a new vulnerability that made him feel guilty as hell for all the things he'd done wrong in his life that had caused her anxiety and stress. He leaned over to kiss her cheek. "I checked all your test and lab results. Has your cardiologist been in to talk to you about it?"

"Yes. But I'd like to hear what you think."

She wanted to hear what he thought? Since when? "You have some mild blockage in your right coronary artery. They're going to do angioplasty to cross through the area that's narrowed by cholesterol plaque, and put in a stent to bridge that narrowing. The procedure has been done for years now, and results are usually good. So, assuming it goes well, you should be your old, bossy self soon."

"I'm never bossy. I'm simply assertive and direct."

"Rafael!"

He turned at the sound of his father's booming voice to see him striding into the room. Unlike Rafael's mother, he looked exactly like he always did, posture erect and the picture of health with his skin tanned from golfing and his silver hair thick and wavy. But his eyes held a worry Rafael had never seen before.

His father's arms enfolded him in a hard hug. "What do you think about your mother? Is she going to be all right? Is what they want to do a good idea? I've talked to the doctors here, but I trust you to know what's really going on."

Rafael stared at him in shock. Again, this was entirely new. He couldn't remember the last time they'd trusted him about anything, let alone his doctoring skills.

"I was just explaining the test results to Mother." He repeated what he'd told her, and as he stood there, beyond surprised at the intent interest on both his parents' faces as he spoke, Gabriella's words came back to him. Saying that he should talk to them, should share how he felt about their opinion of him. He'd told himself for years he didn't care if they respected him or not. But the peculiar mix of emotions filling his chest as he stood there looking at them told him loud and clear he'd been lying to himself.

Maybe Gabriella was right, and it was time to see if the air could be cleared between them, at least a little. "But I have to be honest. I'm surprised you're asking my opinion. You've expressed nothing but disappointment that I decided to become a doctor."

"I admit we wanted you to stay here and help your brother with various royal duties, but when you became a doctor? That wasn't a disappointment, Rafael." His father grasped his shoulder in a strong grip. "We were proud of you."

"Always, Rafael. And I'm sorry we never really told you that," his mother said. Her eyes held some look he couldn't be sure of—guilt, maybe? Contrition? "As I've been lying here, I've thought about you. Realized that perhaps we've been wrong to object to you living your life the way you want to."

"I'm sorry, too," his father said. "In case you don't know, your mother regularly brags about your work. When she's not apologizing for the stupid things you do sometimes, that is." His father's grin took any sting out of his words, and he squeezed Rafael's shoulder before releasing it to hold his mother's hand tight. And when his parents' eyes met both were filled with softness, an obvious connection that he'd never seen between them before.

That rocked him back on his heels as much as what they'd just said. They were proud of him? Even *bragged* about him? He found it nearly impossible to believe, but it was becoming clear he'd been wrong about a lot of things, so maybe it was really true.

His mind filled with a vision of Gabriella and her insight about his family that he hadn't truly thought was a real possibility. Insight that had been pretty incredible, since she hadn't even met his parents. She'd figured out something in just a few minutes of conversation with him that he hadn't seen in thirty-one years.

She was one special woman, no doubt about that. Someone who understood human nature in a way he was obviously still trying to figure out, which was just one reason she was an amazing midwife.

Just one reason why he'd been so attracted to her that very first day they'd met.

A need to talk to her that moment, to call her and tell her he'd taken her advice, had him opening his mouth to tell his parents he'd be back in a short time when a nurse came into the room.

"Time to check your vital signs, Your Majesty," she said, before coming to a dead stop to stare at Rafael.

A good excuse to make his exit. "Then I'll leave you for the moment, Mother. I'll be back in a little while."

He scooted past the nurse, who still hadn't moved, on down the long hallway to an exit door so he'd be sure to get a good signal on his phone. Just the thought of hearing Gabriella's voice made his chest feel lighter than it had since the second his brother had called him in Vail.

Gabby wandered restlessly out of her kitchen with a cup of tea in her hand and plopped onto her sofa. The sofa where she'd made amazing love with Rafael, and thinking of it made her breath short and her heart heavy. If she was going to feel this way every time she sat on it, she might have to sell it and buy a new one. Something a completely different style and color. Maybe rearrange the whole room while she was at it.

Then again, her memories of being in Vail with him—

their hot-air balloon ride, their intimate conversation beneath the stars, their lovemaking there too were all etched in her mind forever. And since being hundreds of miles away from Colorado didn't seem to be doing much to dim those memories, rearranging her living room probably wouldn't help much either.

She grabbed the TV remote and skimmed through some channels, not finding much that grabbed her attention. Why hadn't she taken on a third shift instead of just a double to keep her mind occupied? To keep her mind off Rafael and his mother and wondering how she was and if he was upset and if he'd ever come back to Los Angeles.

Wondering if she'd ever hear from him again.

If she did, she'd try to act normal. Cool. Like the kind of woman he usually dated, who didn't expect anything more than a quick fling. Not that she did expect more than that, or even wanted more than that, and had to somehow make sure he knew that, but still.

Lord, she was a confused mess. She sighed at the same time her phone rang and her heart nearly flipped over in a loop-the-loop when she saw it was him on the line.

"Is your mom okay? Are you okay? Is everything all right? Where are you?"

She winced even as the last words were coming out of her mouth. So much for being calm and cool.

"I'm at the hospital. I've just left Mother for a bit and am glad to say she's doing well. They'll be doing an angioplasty later today, and hopefully that will go smoothly and she'll be heading home soon."

"That's wonderful news! Thanks so much for letting me know. I've been so worried."

"I knew you would be, *bella*, because you care about everyone, even people you've never met. In fact, I have to tell you I took your advice and I'm impressed with your amazing insight. How is it you understand the inner workings of my parents' brains when you don't even know them?"

"What do you mean? What advice?"

"You told me you thought I must be wrong about them not being happy that I became a doctor. And you were right. I just about fell over when they were asking my opinion about Mother's health and the upcoming procedure, and decided then to ask them, to tell them my perspective on it. Only because you'd suggested I do, so I thank you for that. They assured me they aren't unhappy that I became a doctor, and I suspect my relationship with them will be a little less…turbulent now."

"Oh, Rafael. I'm so glad you did." She'd known his parents had to be proud of who he was. How could they not be?

"Me too."

Gabby bit her lip, feeling the silence stretch awkwardly between them but not wanting to say anything that showed how much she'd been missing him. Definitely didn't want to ask what his plans were, and prayed he'd tell her so she wouldn't have to either ask or stay anxiously in the dark about it.

"Anyway, I just wanted to give you an update," he said, his voice low and warm and not all that different from the way it had sounded when they'd made love, and she quivered in spite of herself. "I'm not sure exactly when I'll be back. I'll be staying here at least until she's stabilized from the procedure—I'll let you know how that goes."

"I'd like that. And I'll be thinking of all of you."

"And I'll be thinking of you, Gabriella Cain, both when I'm awake and asleep. You can be sure of that. *Adios* for now."

"Bye." She hoped her voice wasn't shaking at his words as much as her heart was. "Talk to you soon."

She hugged the phone to her chest and grinned like an idiot. Then, seconds later, a niggle of fear jabbed her in the solar plexus. When he came back, would she ready to put herself out there again? Let herself be in a relationship with a man, if that was what he'd been hinting at? Risk getting hurt all over again? There was a part of her that said no. The scared, wimpy part Rafael didn't know about. He thought she was feisty and brave and wasn't that who she wanted to be? Who she used to be?

Rafael had risked his family's disapproval to go for what he wanted, which was to become a doctor. Wasn't the chance to maybe, possibly be happy with him worth even more of a risk?

Yes. There was absolutely no doubt about that. It was worth that and a whole lot more.

She didn't have to be at work for another eight hours. She felt beyond antsy, but it was a little too late to go out somewhere. How in the world was she going to fill the time?

Forty minutes of cleaning her apartment left it unfortunately immaculate. Chewing her lip, she had an *aha* moment. "My knitting stuff and the DVD on how to do it!" Surely learning something new would take up at least an hour, wouldn't it? Then, with any luck, she could get some sleep.

Like that was going to happen.

She pulled the knitting things from a drawer she'd stuffed them into and was crouching down to stick the DVD into the player when one of the shows featuring stories about musicians and movie stars came on the TV. About to switch it off, she stopped dead when Rafael Moreno's face filled the screen.

"And in other news, remember Prince Rafael Moreno and his former stripper girlfriend? Looks like he's gone to the opposite end of the spectrum, dating a wholesome nurse midwife."

Heart pounding, Gabby's legs felt so wobbly that she tumbled back onto her rear as she stared at the bubbly blonde host of the show. How had they found out about her?

"But wholesome and midwife might not always go hand in hand, at least when it comes to Gabriella Cain, who works at the famous and prestigious Hollywood Hills Clinic.

"Our reporters have been busy doing in-depth research on the prince's newest fling and found out that just two years ago she was not only pregnant with another man's child but her utter disregard for her health led to her child being stillborn. A tragedy that could have been avoided, sources say, if she'd been focused on her unborn child instead of herself.

"Not something you would expect from a midwife who takes care of pregnant women every day, is it? We're the first to bring you this breaking report and we are pretty sure that Rafael's parents, and many others in the palace, will be furious all over again about his taste in women. After all, someone like Gabriella Cain isn't the best choice to be the prince's girlfriend or future wife, is she?"

A sickening, icy numbness crept across every inch of Gabby's skin as she watched and listened. Saw the photos of her and Rafael together coming out of his house the morning after the night she'd fallen asleep. Photos at the charity ball. Photos in Vail. Heard the lies, and the truth too, about her mistakes and her loss and how Ben had left her because of her terrible choices. There was even a photo of her baby's grave marker, and seeing it made her feel like she was dying inside.

She was shaking so badly it hurt physically, but she found she couldn't move to turn it off. Had to watch the entire train wreck of her life unfold in garish Technicolor for all the world to see. And just when she was sure it couldn't get any worse, it did.

Because some person, she had no idea who, was offering a loud opinion that someone like Gabby, a woman who'd neglected to pay attention to signs there might be a problem with her own pregnancy and baby, was totally unsuited to be a midwife anywhere, let alone at The Hollywood Hills Clinic, where patients had come to expect the very best.

Dear God.

She should have told Rafael. Should have told him their night together in Vail, when she'd only touched on the truth, telling him about Ben. Had decided she would when the time was right, if there'd been a time that was right. If she'd seen him again.

And now he'd find out this way. In this horrible, lurid, appalling way with exaggerated detail that made her sound like a monster. Not a woman who'd made a bad mistake and had had her heart broken because of it.

She had no idea if Rafael had planned for them to possibly be together as a couple, but it didn't matter. Even if he had, after he heard about this he'd drop that thought fast and run as far as he could. And as she stared at the screen, the nasty things being said about her sounded very far away. A light year's distance.

The same distance she now felt between herself and Rafael.

It made her realize that, even though she hadn't let herself admit it, deep inside her stupid, lonely heart she'd thought maybe, possibly the two of them had something special. Something that might bud into a real relationship, even bloom into a forever-after. But her pathetic heart should have known better than to keep clinging to those Cinderella dreams.

As a prince, the man would surely need an heir. And even if, somehow, he still wanted to be with her after all this, it would be impossible. She could never go through the nightmare of losing a baby again. Never get pregnant again. Because the pain ripping through her heart at that moment felt, impossibly, even more torturous than the day she'd held her beautiful, lifeless baby in her arms.

A damp saltiness touched her lips, and she realized tears were streaking down her cheeks in stinging waterfalls. With shaking hands she slowly swiped them away.

Somehow she had to start a new life. She'd done it two years ago and, as hard as it had been, she could do it again. After this horrifying media exposure she couldn't imagine a single patient would trust her anymore. She didn't want James and Freya to feel bad about having to let her go. And even if, somehow, they didn't want her to leave, she couldn't face the looks and secret whispers about her past and her baby from patients and staff alike, whether it was criticism or sympathy.

No. It was time to cut the cord, so to speak, and be reborn. Again. Start over someplace where people didn't know her past and, somehow, try for a new future.

A future that could never include Rafael, and of all the things ripping out bleeding pieces of her heart that was the very worst.

CHAPTER TWELVE

"RAFAEL!"

His father's bellow carried all the way down the hospital hallway, and Rafael took off in a dead run to his mother's room, fearing the worst. His heart practically stopped when he saw the bed was empty, and his father was pacing the room like an agitated grizzly bear.

"What? Has something happened to Mother?"

"She's all right, for now at least. They took her to prep her for the surgery. I hate to think, though, how your damned latest scandal is going to upset her. The woman has already had a heart attack, Rafael—how is it that you don't care how your actions will affect her recovery? Why don't you give a damn about anyone but yourself?"

"I don't know what you're talking about, but I wouldn't be here if I didn't care about Mother and her health and recovery." He fought down his anger, which was rising to match his father's, because he didn't understand what had enraged the man again.

"You told us you'd go to L.A. to stay out of the news for a while. And now this! Who knows, maybe the last few scandals were part of the reason your mother had her heart attack in the first place. Maybe you should think about her health and recovery first instead of last."

"Again, I don't know what you're talking about, so

please enlighten me." He wanted to add, *Before I put a fist through this wall, or even your face.* Which, of course, he'd never do, but visualizing how good that would feel after being accused, again, of something he doubtless hadn't done helped calm him down.

"This." His father flicked on the TV, and a news station blared with chatter and photos. Rafael stared in horror. These pictures weren't dim and blurred. These showed him holding Gabriella's hand as he'd helped her from the car outside the charity ball. The two of them going into her apartment afterwards. The two of them kissing—hotly kissing—by that fire pit in Vail.

Damn it to hell.

"So I dated a woman? A nice woman. A few casual dates. Since when is that an embarrassment that would give Mother another heart attack?" He tried to keep his voice cool, but it was hard with his breath short and his anger flaming higher. Did his parents expect him to stop living?

"Nice? Not according to this. This shows why she's not a good choice for you. Are you ever going to find someone to settle down with and marry who's appropriate? Who would make your mother happy and proud?"

Proud. There was that word. They'd said they were proud of him for being a doctor, but obviously it stopped there. They weren't proud of his private life, of who he was outside the hospital. He'd told himself he didn't care but, like the rest of it, knew now that wasn't true.

He shifted his gaze back to the TV monitor and listened to the story in all its garishness, his gut burning and his heart feeling like someone had driven a scalpel straight through it.

A stillborn child. This was the source of the pain he'd seen on Gabriella's face as she'd watched little Skye in the incubator. When new mothers had held their infants close to their breasts. And now all that pain was being blasted out there for all the world to see. Lurid details he knew had to be killing her to hear and see splashed in the media, and even unbelievable, nasty comments implying she was unfit to be a midwife.

And that it was happening at all was completely his fault.

His fault. There was no doubt he'd made the torment she obviously carried inside even worse. And as bad as that felt, there was something else digging a hole into his chest. The fact that she hadn't told him any of this, hadn't shared it when they'd been talking about their pasts and their secrets, made him wonder if there were other things in her past she didn't want to share. Other things she wanted to keep hidden.

It seemed most everyone he got involved with had a past that was better left buried. Over and over, his notoriety ended up causing whatever it was to become unearthed. And that hurt everyone. His mother, now ill and fragile. His father, angry about that, and who could blame him? Whatever woman Rafael had been seeing at any moment. And even his career, when a few scandals had threatened to derail his reputation as a doctor, making a few people see only that part of him, and not his skills as a physician.

No wonder he ended up being a disappointment to some of the people closest to him. And not only because of the media. Because he'd never wanted to commit to anyone. Still didn't believe in love and forever-after, though for a brief moment being with Gabriella had made him wonder if he could possibly be wrong about that. He had learned not to fully trust anyone, and felt ashamed that a small part of him felt that way about Gabriella, wondering what might come out next that would upset his mother while she was in Intensive Care. And what kind of son would risk his mother's health and recovery for a fling?

God. What did it say about him that he would even let that cross his mind about Gabriella? Obviously, he couldn't see her anymore. For her sake. For his mother's. The damned selfish man inside him argued with that decision, but Rafael resolutely struck him down. Gabriella had already been through so much terrible heartache. She deserved someone who knew how to trust completely. Who wouldn't expose her to public scandal. A man who could offer her something she might believe was real love, forever wiping away the pain of her old boyfriend leaving just when she'd needed him.

"No, Father, I'm never going to settle down and get married, which I've told you before. I'm sorry that's a disappointment to you and Mother, but that's just the way it is. I'm going to stay here for a while, though, until Mother gets well. Because I do care about her, even though you've thought some of the things I've done make it seem like I don't."

He turned and left the room, heading back to the door opening to the outside, needing to suck some air into his lungs that wasn't vibrating with anger. And to call Gabriella again.

His last promise to his father would be the easiest to keep. Staying away from women wouldn't be an issue, because he had no desire to date anyone besides Gabriella or make love with anyone other than her. And he knew that would be true for a long, long time.

Rafael wasn't sure how long he stood there on the small hospital balcony, staring across the landscape of the place where he'd grown up. The place he'd left for too long, searching for something. When he'd met Gabriella, a part of him, an unconscious part, had felt a little like he might have found it. But that part was the selfish part, and he was kicking that guy out of his life for good.

He knew he needed to stay here for now. Lie low. Really lie low this time, being the poster boy for a good prince doing his duties. Even embrace the good that might come of that, bringing his knowledge of healthcare needs around the world to charitable work here at home. Be here for his mother, keep an eye on her medical care as her health improved. Not upset her. Be here for his family.

He held his phone in his hand, staring at it, but couldn't make himself phone her. He'd ended things with a woman more times than he could count, but it had never felt painful like this did. Nearly impossible, in fact. But he couldn't be the man she needed. He couldn't be his old, selfish self.

He made himself phone her number. It went straight to voice mail, and his heart fell when he realized he wouldn't get to hear her voice again. At the same time, the cowardly part of him felt relieved to be able to just leave a message.

He hesitated over what to say, then decided to keep it short. Without detail, or comments about her pain that he'd just learned about. Anything that might hurt her more, or make her try to contact him. Weaken his resolve to keep her safe from him.

"Gabriella? Rafael. Listen, I'm… Mother is so far still fine, so don't be worried about that, but…well, I don't think I'll be coming back to L.A. I need to stay here until she's stronger. It was great knowing you, and I wish you only the best for your life. Truly." His voice shook on that word, but he couldn't help it. The last ones he whispered, so she wouldn't know. *"Adios, mi bella."*

Gabby sat on the damp, green grass in the Seattle cemetery, not caring that her pants were getting wet and cold.

She couldn't care about her clothes or anything else when she'd lost everything she cared about all over again.

Her baby lay under this earth where she'd just placed a small bouquet of spring tulips. The pain of losing him had slowly faded with time, and even more in the past weeks when she'd realized that shutting herself in a box by working all the time was no way to honor the tiny, beautiful baby who had been her son. Who should have had a chance to grow up into a boy and then a man. Seeing Rafael live his life on his own terms had opened her eyes to the realization that she wanted to live the same way. Without hiding, without fear of what others might think of her if they learned the truth.

But, oh, how wrong she'd been that could be possible. Her past mistake would always be there. Ben had blamed her, and she'd blamed herself. Now others did too, and she thought maybe they were right. Maybe she wasn't fit to be a midwife anymore. A woman who didn't listen to her own body probably shouldn't be listening to anyone else's.

So if she couldn't be a midwife anymore, where did she belong? What would she do with her life? God, she just didn't know. But she did know one thing. She could never be a wife and mother, because there was no way she could go through that kind of heartache all over again. She'd gone back into hiding from that, at least, and this time she was never coming out.

Staring down at the small stone carved with her baby's name, she became aware of a movement next to her and turned her head, only to have her heart completely stop in shock.

Ben.

For a moment she could barely process it. She opened her mouth to speak, but nothing came out. He gave her a twisted smile then knelt on the grass next to her. "Hi, Gabby. Rough day, huh?"

He'd seen the news. "Yeah. Pretty rough."

"All that garbage on TV made me think about you and this little guy. Gave me a strangely strong need to come here, and now that I see you're here too, I figure that's the reason why."

"What do you mean?"

"Because the universe knows I need to make things right with you."

"Make what right?"

He stared at her a long moment, his hand gripping the back of his neck before he dropped it, placing it on top of hers. "Hell. I…I'd been thinking that maybe I'd call you after I stopped here today, but now that you're right in front of me, all the things I know I should say to you seem a lot harder than I thought they would."

Since she didn't have any idea what to say to him either, she kept quiet and just looked at him, waiting. Bracing herself for the worst.

"I know I treated you badly when our baby died inside of you," he finally said. "I was hurt at losing him and angry at the world about it. I took that anger out on you."

"No, you didn't. You didn't say much about anything." And in some ways that terrible silence, his inability to talk about it, had been worse to take than if he'd ranted at her.

"Maybe not. But when you blamed yourself I didn't tell you it wasn't your fault. I felt the same horrible loss you did, and it pushed me to act in a way I'm not proud of. I let you believe I blamed you, but I never did. Not really."

Again, she didn't respond, having no idea how to process what he was saying. How to feel about it. She'd held his blame, along with her own, so close to her bruised and battered heart. Had let it live there, a sharp splinter that had stabbed and festered, and she hadn't even tried to remove it because she'd believed she deserved the pain.

"There's more, and I want to tell you about it," he continued, still wearing that wry smile. "I'm married now. Have a baby on the way, and after what happened to us I admit I've been damned scared. I've asked her doctor lots of questions, and he's explained things to me. So even if there was a part of me that wasn't sure back then, I know now. You working late that day, assuming the pains you felt were nothing? That didn't have a damned thing to do with losing our baby. It was just one of those really bad outcomes that happen sometimes."

Gabby's throat closed, and tears burned the backs of her eyes as she looked at Ben. The man who two years ago she'd expected to share her life with. Who had in one second of hardship left.

This was proof he was the good person she'd thought he was. That he'd been perhaps as immature and unprepared as she'd been in trying to deal with their loss. "Thank you for telling me this. It's been…very hard to know how to feel about it."

"I know. But here's something else I want to tell you. We both had a bad time of it, but I've finally found happiness again. I love my wife and can't wait until our baby is born. I don't know what's going on with you and this prince guy in the news, but you know…?" His smile broadened to become a real one. "It's worth taking a risk. It is. And he'd be one lucky guy to have you."

Unable to say another word, stunned by all he'd said, Gabby just stared at him. He reached out to squeeze her shoulder before he stood, and after a lingering look at their baby's headstone he was gone.

Gabby sat for long minutes, processing it all. The knowledge that he didn't blame her seeped slowly into the fog in her brain. Pushed out some of the guilt she'd carried for so long. And as that guilt eased from her chest it was replaced by cautious optimism.

Maybe she could put the past behind her, the way Ben had. Maybe she could be happy again, and maybe that happiness could come from being with Rafael. Hadn't she decided, before the shock of the media mess, that she needed to try to be more like her old self? That spending time with him to see where it might lead was worth the risk of future pain?

A gusty breeze moved her hair, and she had to smile. She could feel it. A shift in the wind, both literally and figuratively. No more guilt. No more hiding. No more self-protection. Time to move on, and what better way than to reach for the hand of a certain handsome prince who, from what he'd told her about his relationship with his parents, just might be experiencing a little shift in the wind himself?

She looked down at the small gravestone. She kissed her fingertips then slowly caressed the name and date etched there before standing tall. As she walked to her car she knew that part of this healing, part of moving forward would come from sharing everything with Rafael. Talking about it over the phone wouldn't be the way to do it, but with any luck his mother would improve and he'd be back soon.

Her chest filling with a buoyancy she hadn't felt in a long, long time, Gabby fished her keys from her purse and got into the car. Then her heart smacked into her ribs when she saw Rafael had called and left a message.

A giddy feeling of joy bubbled through her, and she quickly brought up her voice mail. His voice was odd, not warm like it usually was. Not even filled with its normal confidence, and in seconds the bubble deflated and flattened completely.

Her ears rang as she listened to the classic brush-off. "It was great knowing you, and I wish you only the best for your life..." Then his final quiet words felt like a hard slap of reality. *"Adios, mi bella."*

Adios, mi bella.

She wasn't sure how long she sat in the car, hands still holding the phone limply in her lap. Her pants, damp from the grass, now chilled her to the bone, and somehow she finally managed to lift her hands to the steering wheel to get the engine running and the heat on.

What a fool she was. Thinking Rafael, a man who'd stated more than once that he didn't believe in long-term relationships and forever-after, would want to be with her longer than a few days or weeks. But even as that knowledge felt like a huge hole in her heart she straightened her spine. Looked into the rearview mirror, swiped away the tears leaking from her eyes, and saw the new Gabby. A stronger Gabby. A woman who was moving on from the past to a new future. A person who deserved someone who loved her—hadn't Ben said any man would be lucky to have her? She'd thought maybe Rafael was that man, but that had been a pipe dream. A fairy tale.

Her cold hands gripped the steering wheel. Once she found a new job she'd find a way to balance work with finding a life that included other things. Maybe she'd even get lucky like Ben and find someone to love who'd love her back.

The hardest thing she'd ever done had been dealing with the loss of her baby. The next hardest thing?

Forgetting all about Rafael Moreno.

CHAPTER THIRTEEN

"So you agree that your mother looks good? That she's recovering well?"

Rafael looked at the anxiety in his father's eyes as they walked to his mother's room, surprised all over again at the intensity of it. Though he supposed he shouldn't be. Even if his parents didn't have a particularly close relationship, they'd still been married for over thirty-five years, so that had to mean something.

"The angioplasty went well, and every test so far shows she's doing very well. I'm sure they told you they're planning to release her tomorrow for some T.L.C. back at the palace."

"Yes. But I wanted to make sure you agreed with that."

Just yesterday, his father's words would have pleased him. At that moment, though, he didn't seem able to feel much more than a heavy emptiness. "I agree with it. I'm guessing you've scheduled more nursing care than she wants, and she'll be chafing at the bit about everyone fussing around her."

His father chuckled. "She's already chafing. You know your mother."

They entered the room, and his mother promptly frowned at him. "You're giving me that disapproving look," he said. "Never thought I'd miss it, but at least it shows you're feeling pretty good."

"I'm wondering what's happened with your latest scandal. Really, Rafael, it's unbelievable."

"Why do you always pick the wrong women, son?" his father chimed in. "It's like you do it on purpose."

He stared at his father. Maybe he did. Maybe he'd always chosen women he knew were "inappropriate" as part of keeping his distance from them. But Gabriella? He hadn't really chosen her.

He'd been irresistibly drawn to her.

"Maybe I've done that in the past, Father, but Gabriella Cain is different from any woman I've ever known." He might not be able to be with her again, but he wasn't about to tolerate anyone saying nasty things about her. "She's not only beautiful, she's smart and good at her job and beyond caring to her patients. I don't know the whole story the media's been throwing out there, but I do know it has to be sensationalized and maybe even totally wrong. If you met Gabriella, you'd love her."

His mother's frown lifted into raised eyebrows, and she cocked her head. "Sounds like maybe *you* love her."

He stilled. Pictured Gabriella's sweet face and fiery hair and the tenderness in her eyes, and knowing he'd never see any of that again physically hurt.

Love her? Maybe he did. What he felt for her was unlike anything he'd felt before. But love was fleeting, he knew.

Both his parents were looking at him expectantly, but he didn't want to talk about Gabriella unless he had to, and changed the subject. "How does the surgical entry wound feel, Mother? Has the pain lessened?"

"Yes. It's not too bad."

"I've seen them change the bandages, and it looks bad to me," his father said. "Your mother's just tough. Always has been." As he looked at his wife the man's eyes were filled with a warmth and softness Rafael had rarely seen.

"Is that a compliment or something else?" His mother reached for his father's hand and smiled at him.

"A compliment. As though I'd give anything else to my very special wife." He held her hand tight, leaning to give her forehead a lingering kiss.

Rafael stared at the way his parents looked at one another. At the…the *love* in his father's eyes as he gently stroked her skin, bruised from the needle sticks and IV.

His parents *did* love each other? Even though their marriage had been arranged and the time they spent together seemed to be far less than the time they spent apart? All Rafael had ever noticed had been cordial respect between them, but maybe because they were his own parents he hadn't really been looking.

All those questions and revelations jumbled around in his head until everything settled into a new order and a clear focus. And with that focus came another vision of Gabriella.

Until this very second, once his mother was completely well, he'd planned to keep living his life the way he always had, moving from place to place and from woman to woman and from job to job. Never dipping his toe deeper than the shallow end of the pool for fear of becoming trapped and emotionally entangled, ending up in a long-term loveless situation like his parents and brother.

Except, apparently, he'd been wrong about that. And could that mean he might be wrong about his sibling's marriage too?

It didn't really matter. What mattered was that he'd closed his mind and heart to any possibility of real love. Had shut it tight, not even realizing he'd been doing it. But wanting to see inside Gabriella's heart and mind for the time he was with her had cracked his heart and brain open instead, just enough to let in a sliver of light. Instead of learning her secrets, she'd gently but directly gotten him to spill his own. To explain that he was the black sheep and always would be. Instead of judging him, she'd believed in him. Believed his parents must, too.

And he was damned if she hadn't been absolutely right.

He watched his father cup his mother's cheek in his palm, and their stunning love and deep connection struck him all over again.

At that moment he knew he looked at Gabriella exactly the same way. Looked at her in a way he'd never before looked at a woman, and if he was as lucky as hell, she just might look back at him the same way. He didn't have to worry about protecting her from him, because she'd turned him into a different man. He didn't have to worry about exposing her to media rumors, because he was ready to make a commitment to her he'd never dreamed possible until now.

"I'm in love with her." He actually said the words out loud he was so shocked. And rocked back onto his heels yet again.

"What did you say?"

He blinked to see both his parents looking at him quizzically. "I said I'm in love with her. Gabriella Cain. I'm in love with her, and I'd like to talk to you about it."

Normally, on a long flight Rafael could get some sleep in the comfortable bed on his family's jet. But that had proved impossible. He'd read medical journals he needed to catch up on, checked the stock market, and even worked on some crossword puzzles, which he hadn't done in years. But no matter what he did, his mind was only partly there. Gabriella occupied most of his thoughts, and all of his heart, and every hour that passed before he could tell her how she'd changed him and ask her to be his wife felt like extended torture.

Finally, the early evening lights of L.A. stretched across the horizon and he found himself wondering which golden light, of the millions of lights switching on at that moment in the city, was the one lighting her cozy living room.

The jet's wheels had barely touched the runway when he switched on his cellphone to call her. He saw that he had a voice-mail message from James, and, much as he was desperate to talk to Gabriella, figured he should find out what James wanted, in case it had something to do with her. When he pulled it up to listen to it, he stopped smiling and stopped breathing at the same time.

Then listened to it again.

"Rafael, it's James. Do you happen to know where Gabby went? Give me a call."

What the hell? What did James mean?

He quickly punched in her number, and a cold dread began to seep through his veins when a recorded message said the number was no longer in service. He stared hard at the phone as if, somehow, he could reach inside to conjure Gabriella straight out of it.

What had he said in his voice-mail message to her? He couldn't remember exactly, but he didn't think it was anything that would have made her take off. Was it? Which probably meant, if she'd left L.A., it was because the horrible media story had driven her away.

If she was hurting and gone, the blame lay squarely at his feet and, damn it, he was going to make it right.

As the jet taxied down the runway, Rafael called James, cursing when he didn't answer. It seemed forever before the jet had parked and he could leave it to run to his car, which he'd arranged to have dropped off there for him. If

Gabriella had been nervous about the speed he'd driven in the mountains, she'd have closed her eyes for sure if she'd been in the car with him now, taking curves like the devil was on his heels. And he could practically feel it nipping, because a deep sense of foreboding had filled his chest. A feeling that this wasn't going to be as simple as showing up at her door, sweeping her into his arms and telling her that her past didn't matter and that he would always be there for her.

He skidded to a stop in front of her apartment and banged on her door. But of course there was no answer. Was she in there, or had she gone? He should have called James to see if he'd come here looking for her. He banged some more, until her neighbor's door opened.

"What's all the racket out here?" the man asked.

"Do you know if Gabriella Cain is home?"

"Saw her leave yesterday. Had a few suitcases with her."

Damn it! "Thanks." Rafael spun on his heel and pushed his car even harder to get to the clinic, parking it practically sideways before he ran inside.

Desperately hoping that somehow she'd shown back up after James had left his message, he checked her office first but it was quiet and empty. Now it was just a room, with all the life and energy gone from it. He put his hands on her desk and leaned on it, needing that support when he saw that her usual tidy stacks of papers were gone, and so were the few personal items he'd noticed there before.

"She handed in her resignation."

Rafael swung around at the sound of James's voice. His friend stood there looking grim and angry, rubbing the back of his neck with his palm.

"When?"

"Yesterday. That's why I'm here so late, trying to find a replacement. Not that it'll be easy to replace someone like Gabby. I've been trying like hell to figure out where she went so I could talk her into coming back, but no luck so far."

"Why did she leave?"

"Because the damned news outlets were splashing photos of the two of you everywhere, and along with that some people were running their mouths about her past making her unfit to work here as a midwife. I'm tempted to call the news outlets who've run this damned story, but since they're always looking for a way to throw the media spotlight on me, too, I'm afraid it would just make it worse. Did you warn her this could happen if the two of you spent time together?"

"Not enough, obviously." Damn it, this was what he'd wanted to avoid all along, and he should have told her about the grainy photos from that first night together, when she'd fallen asleep at his house. Maybe she'd have been more prepared for this if she'd known they'd been dogging both of them from the start.

But things were different now. She wasn't just another fling, she was the woman he loved. He'd be more than happy to have that be headline news, if she loved him back.

The thought that she might not made it hard to breathe.

"I'm going to get with some of my people from the palace. See if they can find out where she's from, where her family is, or who her old friends are. I'll start there."

"All I know is that she's from Seattle. I'll keep working on it and let you know. I want her back too. Good luck."

James gave Rafael a quick, hard hug, then left and Rafael sat in Gabriella's chair to get started on the most important hunt of his life.

Gabby sat on the dock near her childhood home and stared out at the Pacific Ocean, pulling her jacket closer around her to keep away the penetrating evening chill. Always, whenever she'd had problems in her life, she'd felt soothed by the sound of the surf. By watching the rhythmic waves slide up and down the sand. By seeing the orange sun gleaming lower in the sky to finally dip below the horizon. All of it usually left her feeling like she was ready to take on whatever challenge she had to face.

Her current challenge, forgetting about Rafael Moreno, felt pretty impossible. Taking the positive step to begin sending out applications for jobs had helped a little. Maybe once she moved somewhere to start afresh, met new people and didn't hide away like she had the two years she'd been at The Hollywood Hills Clinic, it would get better. Maybe forgetting him would be easier than she expected.

And maybe the seagulls would start swimming and fish would fly across the sky.

A sigh filled her chest. Surprised by a movement next to her, she looked up, and her heart ground to a complete halt.

"So, *querida*, you are here." Rafael dropped down next to her, and in his quiet voice was a note she hadn't heard before. "Should you ever become a felon, be glad to know you're very hard to find."

"Rafael. How…? Why…? Is your mother okay?" Her heart started up again in lurching thuds against her ribs, and she just stared in disbelief that he was actually there. And why, when he'd given her the brush-off and basically said goodbye, have a nice life?

"My mother is fine. Tell me why you left L.A." He reached for her hand, but she pulled it away. Somehow he couldn't have seen what was on TV.

She licked her lips, and her gut churned with dread, but she had to tell him. "The media ran a story. About me, and…and how I gave birth to my stillborn son. Talked about how I should have done things differently. Why I shouldn't be a midwife and…it's all true. Except that it wasn't my fault. I realize that now, and I know I'm still good at what I do."

"I know. I heard the story." He reached for her again, and this time she let his warm hand engulf her frozen one. "Of course you're still good at what you do. Better than good. I'm so sorry this difficult part of your life has been thrown out there for all the world to see. It's all my fault, and I feel very badly about that."

So that was why he was here. To apologize for the media, which wasn't really his fault at all.

She stared back at the horizon because she couldn't bear to look at his face. "I don't think it's your fault any more than my losing the baby was mine. Don't worry, I'll cope."

"I know that too. You're a strong woman, not to mention talented and caring and so beautiful you make me ache." He took her face in his hands, the green eyes meeting hers filled with tenderness as he turned her toward him. "Tell me about your baby. Tell me what happened."

God, she didn't want to talk about it. But maybe telling the story would be part of the process to continue to heal. To truly put it in the past. "I was working late. Had finished a long shift, and my patient had been in labor a long time. She was very upset and exhausted, and even though I'd been feeling odd pains all evening I really felt I should stay with her, be there for her until her baby was born. She developed complications and ended up having surgery, and I couldn't just leave her with an OB she'd never met before. So I stayed, and her baby was born healthy."

She closed her eyes, not wanting to remember the rest of it. Rafael's hands slipped to her shoulders as he rested his cheek against hers. "And then what happened?"

"By then I was feeling really bad. I went to my office, and the pain was so overwhelming I collapsed. By the time someone found me I was in premature labor." She pulled her cheek from his and opened her eyes, barely able to squeeze out the rest of the story. "I'll never forget the moment when they listened for his heartbeat, but there wasn't one. They attached the monitor to be sure, but nothing. My baby was dead. I had to deliver him, knowing he was gone. And never, as long as I live, will I forget how it felt to hold his small, motionless body in my arms, eyes closed, an incredibly peaceful look on his tiny, perfect face. The face of an angel."

Her voice broke as the memories flooded her. Rafael had said she was strong. Now he knew otherwise.

"I'm so sorry," he said, folding her close against him. She let herself cling to him for a long moment. Pressed her face to his neck. Let herself soak in his warmth one last time. "I've delivered stillborn babies, and I've seen the parents' pain. I can't imagine it. But I'm glad to hear you know it wasn't your fault. That probably your baby wasn't growing normally. Most likely, your pains came after he had passed away inside you, and whether or not you'd gone to see someone earlier about it wouldn't have made any difference."

His hand stroking slowly up and down her back felt even more soothing than watching the ocean. "I know. I do. But it's hard not to feel like somehow, if I'd done things differently, he'd be here now."

She could feel his face move against her hair in what she took to be a nod before he pulled back. "Thank you for sharing this with me. Now I'd like to share with you the second reason I'm here."

His face was so serious she readied herself for some other thing even worse than the first media blitz, though surely that wasn't possible. "What is it?"

"I'd decided I should stay at home for a while. Figured

I'd been running from there for too long and hurting others in the process." His wide palms cupped her face again. "Hurting you, both with the media focus and because I knew I couldn't give you the kind of love you deserve."

Oh, God. And here he was, hurting her now by stating the obvious. She tried to turn away from him, but he held her gaze.

"Then I found I was wrong. Again. I've been wrong about so damn many things, but the biggest was believing that there's no such thing as real love. Lasting love. I know I was wrong because I'm very much in love with you, Gabriella. And I know that I'll love you forever."

"Rafael." Her heart thundered in her ears so loudly it drowned out the sound of the ocean waves. What was he saying, exactly?

"I love you. Like I've never loved anyone before." This time he whispered the words. "And I hope and pray that, even though I sure as hell don't deserve it, you might love me back."

Tears stung her eyes and spilled over, and his thumbs slowly slid across her cheeks to wipe them away.

"I do love you. But it's me who doesn't deserve you. And someday you'll want children. Will need an heir for your country. I don't think I can go through losing a baby again."

"I don't need to produce an heir. My brother's wife is expecting as we speak, and since I know she wants a big brood, there will be more than enough Morenos running around the palace to satisfy the entire kingdom."

That vision managed to make her smile a little, even through her tears, because she could just see green-eyed, dark-haired Morenos who looked like Rafael, loudly tearing up and down marble hallways and breaking priceless antiquities. And with that vision came the longing again to have a child, but hadn't she gone through enough pain already?

He must have seen something in her face, because his usual arrogant confidence seemed to be on shaky ground as he drew her closer. "The only thing I need in my life is you, Gabriella. I need you to help me see things I can't otherwise see on my own, except through your beautiful eyes. And because my parents are happy that I'm crazily in love with a wonderful woman, and thrilled at the thought of me never again embarrassing them, they gave me something to give to you. If you'll accept it."

The tenderness and intensity and even a shocking vulnerability in his eyes stole her breath, and it took her two attempts to find her voice. "Accept what?"

"This thing in my pocket that's digging into my ribs, and I hope you'll help me relieve my pain." His fingers stroked her cheeks once more before leaving them to pull a surprisingly worn-looking box from his jacket.

"That looks about a hundred years old," she said through sniffles she knew had to be awfully unattractive, but she couldn't seem to do a thing about the tears that kept leaking from her eyes.

"Four hundred, actually. My great-great…some big number of greats-grandmother was given this ring by some great-great-grandfather." He surprised her by folding his fingers back around the box, and she nearly begged him to let her at least look inside. His other fingers tipped her chin up to meet his eyes. "Will you marry me, Gabriella? Be my wife? My princess? Please say yes."

Gabby stared, unable to fully process his words, unable to speak, and he pressed his lips softly to hers before pulling back again. "You're scaring me here, Gabriella. Will it help to see the ring?"

He flipped open the box, and she gasped at the huge, square-cut emerald surrounded by diamonds. An emerald that dazzled almost as much as Rafael's eyes. As Rafael himself. But not quite.

"It's beautiful," she whispered, "but I didn't need to see it to say yes. Yes, I love you and, yes, I'll marry you."

"Thank God," he whispered back. He pulled her close, and she could feel his body relax as he pressed his cheek to hers. "I promise you won't regret it. I'll do everything I can to make you happy."

Long seconds ticked by as they just held one another, and she knew he was feeling the same unbelievable connection radiating between them without another spoken word. When they slowly parted, he pulled the ring from the box and slipped it onto her finger. As she looked down at it, a bubble of happiness ballooned in her chest so big she thought she might just float away. At the same time she realized there was one important thing they hadn't talked about.

"I assume you want to go back to your country to live? Would I…if we're married…be able to work?"

"I'm not going to lie," he said, his lips twisting. "Being my wife will require helping with some charitable work I'd like to start in the kingdom, and public appearances. But we can live anywhere you want, and you can do whatever you want, including be a midwife. We can work together, if you like, or not. It's up to you."

"I don't know. You can be awfully overbearing and bossy."

"Another reason I need feisty and amazing Gabriella to keep me in my place." He gave her another lingering kiss then stood, holding out his hand to help her to her feet. "What do you say we go back to L.A. for now, until we make a plan?"

"Yes." She twined her fingers with his, hardly able to believe this was really happening. "I think I'm finally ready to move on to wherever life takes me next. With you."

CHAPTER FOURTEEN

"HERE'S SOME NEWS I think you'll want to read with your breakfast, Gabriella," Rafael said, sliding several newspapers in front of her on the table.

"I'm enjoying being pampered by you in this beautiful house." She scowled and took a fortifying swig of the delicious coffee Rafael had made. "Why would you want to ruin that for me by making me read the news?"

"I don't think this news will ruin your morning." He refilled her cup and she looked up to see his lips were curved and his eyes were dancing.

Moving on from her past didn't mean she wanted to read the awful stuff that had continued to be plastered in all the media but she had to admit his expression made her curious. She glanced at the headline and her heart stumbled.

"What…is this?" She slowly picked up the paper, staring.

"The world is defending you, *querida,*" Rafael said. "Shall I read a few of the quotes? *'Gabriella Cain is the best thing to ever happen to The Hollywood Hills Clinic.'* I like that one, since she's definitely the best thing to ever happen to me." He dropped a kiss on her head. "And how about this? *'Anyone who knows midwife Gabriella Cain knows this trash being said about her can't possibly be true.'*"

"Oh, my gosh." She stared up at him, her heart somehow squeezing and swelling at the same time. "This is incredible!"

"And my favorite, from Cameron Fontaine," Rafael continued, flicking through another paper. *"'If Gabriella Cain isn't hired back by The Hollywood Hills Clinic there will be a boycott. And if there isn't an immediate retraction from the media, taking back all those ridiculous and inflammatory statements, influential actresses and studio directors like me are going to sue the hell out of every single one of them.'"*

Gabby put her hands to her cheeks and laughed. "Oh, my gosh, that's so Cameron. I guess she liked me after all."

"Loved you. As I do." He leaned down to kiss her cheek, moving on to her mouth, and just as Gabby was clutching his shirt and sinking into another delicious kiss, the doorbell rang.

"Well, who could that be? Maybe it's the media come to apologize."

"Like that would ever happen." There was something odd, secretive even, about the smile playing on his lips, and Gabby had to wonder why.

"You never know, when a woman like you has so much clout behind her." He winked and headed for the door, and when he returned a moment later a familiar voice came with him.

"Gabby. You've got to help me out," James said. "There's a near-riot at the clinic!"

"A near-riot? What are you talking about?"

"Several of your pregnant patients are refusing to see anyone else, and they're threatening a sit-in if you don't come back. They're mad as hell that you're gone and they're blaming me." James threw his arms wide, and she nearly laughed at the look of alarm on his normally cool, impassive face. "Will you come back? Please? Tell me what it would take and I'll make it happen."

The swelling of her heart grew so much she could barely hold in all her joy. Then remembered she wasn't living her life alone anymore. That there were two of them now. Someday, maybe, she might even be ready to add a few more to the wonderful life she and Rafael would share.

She turned to him, and her face must have told him exactly what she was thinking because he stepped close, pulled her into his arms and kissed her forehead.

"The clinic is a pretty great place to work, isn't it?" He tipped her chin and his beautiful eyes smiled into hers.

"Yes. It is." She pressed her palms against his chest and smiled back. "How would you feel about us both working there?"

"You already know, Gabriella Cain," he said, his warm gaze a steady promise, "that wherever it is you want to be, I'm right there by your side."

* * * * *

Look out for the next great story in
THE HOLLYWOOD HILLS CLINIC

HIS PREGNANT SLEEPING BEAUTY
by Lynne Marshall

And if you missed where it all started, check out

SEDUCED BY THE HEART SURGEON
by Carol Marinelli

FALLING FOR THE SINGLE DAD
by Emily Forbes

TEMPTED BY HOLLYWOOD'S TOP DOC
by Louisa George

PERFECT RIVALS...
by Amy Ruttan

All available now!
And there are two more fabulous stories to come...

MILLS & BOON®

Hardback – June 2016

ROMANCE

Bought for the Greek's Revenge	Lynne Graham
An Heir to Make a Marriage	Abby Green
The Greek's Nine-Month Redemption	Maisey Yates
Expecting a Royal Scandal	Caitlin Crews
Return of the Untamed Billionaire	Carol Marinelli
Signed Over to Santino	Maya Blake
Wedded, Bedded, Betrayed	Michelle Smart
The Surprise Conti Child	Tara Pammi
The Greek's Nine-Month Surprise	Jennifer Faye
A Baby to Save Their Marriage	Scarlet Wilson
Stranded with Her Rescuer	Nikki Logan
Expecting the Fellani Heir	Lucy Gordon
The Prince and the Midwife	Robin Gianna
His Pregnant Sleeping Beauty	Lynne Marshall
One Night, Twin Consequences	Annie O'Neil
Twin Surprise for the Single Doc	Susanne Hampton
The Doctor's Forbidden Fling	Karin Baine
The Army Doc's Secret Wife	Charlotte Hawkes
A Pregnancy Scandal	Kat Cantrell
A Bride for the Boss	Maureen Child

0516 GEN STD HB

MILLS & BOON®

Hardback – July 2016

ROMANCE

Di Sione's Innocent Conquest	Carol Marinelli
Capturing the Single Dad's Heart	Kate Hardy
The Billionaire's Ruthless Affair	Miranda Lee
A Virgin for Vasquez	Cathy Williams
Master of Her Innocence	Chantelle Shaw
Moretti's Marriage Command	Kate Hewitt
The Flaw in Raffaele's Revenge	Annie West
The Unwanted Conti Bride	Tara Pammi
Bought by Her Italian Boss	Dani Collins
Wedded for His Royal Duty	Susan Meier
His Cinderella Heiress	Marion Lennox
The Bridesmaid's Baby Bump	Kandy Shepherd
Bound by the Unborn Baby	Bella Bucannon
Taming Hollywood's Ultimate Playboy	Amalie Berlin
Winning Back His Doctor Bride	Tina Beckett
White Wedding for a Southern Belle	Susan Carlisle
Wedding Date with the Army Doc	Lynne Marshall
The Baby Inheritance	Maureen Child
Expecting the Rancher's Child	Sara Orwig
Doctor, Mummy...Wife?	Dianne Drake

0616 GEN STD HB

MILLS & BOON®

Large Print – July 2016

ROMANCE

The Italian's Ruthless Seduction	Miranda Lee
Awakened by Her Desert Captor	Abby Green
A Forbidden Temptation	Anne Mather
A Vow to Secure His Legacy	Annie West
Carrying the King's Pride	Jennifer Hayward
Bound to the Tuscan Billionaire	Susan Stephens
Required to Wear the Tycoon's Ring	Maggie Cox
The Greek's Ready-Made Wife	Jennifer Faye
Crown Prince's Chosen Bride	Kandy Shepherd
Billionaire, Boss...Bridegroom?	Kate Hardy
Married for Their Miracle Baby	Soraya Lane

HISTORICAL

The Secrets of Wiscombe Chase	Christine Merrill
Rake Most Likely to Sin	Bronwyn Scott
An Earl in Want of a Wife	Laura Martin
The Highlander's Runaway Bride	Terri Brisbin
Lord Crayle's Secret World	Lara Temple

MEDICAL

A Daddy for Baby Zoe?	Fiona Lowe
A Love Against All Odds	Emily Forbes
Her Playboy's Proposal	Kate Hardy
One Night...with Her Boss	Annie O'Neil
A Mother for His Adopted Son	Lynne Marshall
A Kiss to Change Her Life	Karin Baine